Reunited
At
Christmas

Debra Ullrick

Reunited at Christmas
Copyright © Debra Ullrick, 2013

Scripture taken from the New King James Version® Copyright © 1982 by Thomas Nelson, Inc. Used by permission. All rights reserved.

Published by: Sweet Impressions Publishing
Cover Design by Lynnette Bonner
Cover images ©BigStock- 53537611, 54003706, 49652564

Printed in the United States of America

Acknowledgements

Jeff Pulliam, thank you for sharing your search and rescue expertise with me. (Author's note: If there are any mistakes regarding this, they are mine, and mine alone.)

Thank you, Kayce Phillips and Julie Blair, for being my "proof readers". I love you both so very dearly.

Thank you, Holy Spirit, for guiding me and for coming alongside me to write this book.

And last, but definitely not least, THANK YOU, STACI STALLINGS. I love you, girl. I'm so blessed that God put you in my life. I have learned so much from you. Not just writing-wise, but spiritually, emotionally, and in all things pertaining to life itself. Thank you for editing my books, for adding your fabulous touches to them, for teaching me how to write, for being such an excellent mentor, and for doing it all with such grace and such patience. You rock!

Dedication

To my friend, Julie Blair, who is always there for me.
Thanks for being such a good listener and
for being such a fabulous friend. I love you, girl.

...the Lord was with him... *Genesis 39:23b*

Chapter One

How could she possibly say no?

A human being's life was at stake.

To make matters worse, that person was Ryker Anderson, the man who had crushed Shelby Davis's heart and dashed her dreams three months before their wedding when he had called to say goodbye to her with no warning and no explanation.

That day ran through her mind like it had millions of times since then.

"Shelby, I've got to leave. I still love you. That's why I have to do this. Please forgive me. Goodbye." The line went dead. She tried to call Ryker back several times, but he didn't answer. She'd gone to his home, and when he didn't come to the door, she let herself in with the spare key he kept hidden under a bush only to discover most of his clothes and possessions were gone.

Fresh pain and anger pressed into her heart as if it had just happened instead of eighteen long months ago. She so desperately wanted to say no to this rescue, but no matter what he had done to her, she wouldn't let that or the thought of seeing him again stop her from saving his life.

With a heavy sigh, Shelby asked her best friend Hailey Marks, "How soon do you want to leave?"

"How soon can you be ready?"

"Fifteen minutes."

"That'll work. You want to pick me up, or do you want me to pick you up?"

"I'll pick you up since I have my sleds already loaded in my trailer. Plus, I'll have Max, and I wouldn't want my dog to mess up the inside of that new pickup of yours."

"I wouldn't want him to either." They both chuckled. Hailey had saved for years to buy a Dodge Ram pickup almost identical to Shelby's. Now that Hailey had finally bought one, Shelby was certain her friend wouldn't want a dog shedding hair all over its brand new interior. "See you in a few, Shelby." With those words Hailey ended the call. No goodbye, no anything. Shelby found it interesting that a lot of her friends never said goodbye, they just hung up. The one person who did say goodbye, she'd never heard from him again.

Oh well, she shrugged, she wasn't going to dwell on that now. There were far more important things she needed to concentrate on at the moment. "C'mon, Max, we've got to hurry."

She gave her blue-merle Australian Shepherd a quick scratch behind the ears. Max's toenails clicked on the glossy knotty pine floor as the two of them headed over to her oversized gear bag near the back door of her family's log home. Her home now, purchased with the royalty money she had made from her bestselling suspense novels.

She loved this charming 2800 square foot home with its powder-blue and white leather furniture and rustic moose, elk, deer, and bear décor. Most of the furniture was either leather or knotty-pine-logwood-style or a combination of the two, like her kitchen table and chairs and matching breakfast nook stools.

That it was nestled in pine trees and within walking distance of the shores of Grand Lake in Grand Lake, Colorado, was what she loved the most about this place. Having a beautiful lake right out her back door was a dream come true. She loved water skiing and boating and anything outdoors. Her mother oftentimes joked that she should have been born a fish because she spent so much time in the water. This place gave her the opportunity to do all the things she loved including snowmobiling. Speaking of snowmobiling, she'd better hurry and get ready.

Shelby knelt next to the powder-blue bag, and Max joined her. She unzipped the thing and made a quick check of its contents.

Probe. Check.

Shovel. Check.

Saw. Check.

Beacon. Check.

Spare clothing and goggles. Check.

Food and water. Check.

Radio. Check.

She continued ticking the items off, making sure everything she would need was in there even though she already knew they were. Still, before going on any rescue run, she liked to double-check things just in case. When she finished, Shelby ran to her room and dressed in her warmest undergarments. She flew down the stairs, put on her powder-blue ski coat and boots, grabbed her bag, and stepped outside, making sure Max was right behind her.

Snowflakes the size of feathers melted against her cheeks. She glanced up at her backyard floodlight. Heavy snowfall swirled and danced in its light. She sighed. Finding someone in this weather was going to be extremely difficult.

Not letting that deter her, she traipsed down the pathway toward the shop where her pickup and snowmobile trailer were housed and marveled at how quickly the walkway had filled in with snow. Only a mere hour before, she had completely cleared it off. And now, it looked like she hadn't done a thing.

Shelby sent up a quick prayer for it to stop snowing so their chances of rescuing Ryker would be greater. Then she sent up another for his safety and good health when they did find him. That one grated across her raw nerves, but she willfully pushed the annoyance away. He was a human being, and he was in trouble. She needed no more motive than that.

Inside her shop, she stomped the snow off her feet, and brushed the snow off her coat before climbing into the cab of her Dodge Ram. She started her pickup to get the engine warmed up and then loaded everything she needed onto the folded-down backseat of her mega-cab.

"Load up, Max." She shifted out of the way so her dog could get in. She gave Max a quick hug, marveling at how blessed she was to be able to do the things she loved. Not only did she write novels, but she trained search and rescue dogs. Max was her best search dog to date.

As a handler, when she had first started training Max, she wasn't sure how well he would do as a pure bred Aussie. Most certified trainers used German Shepherds or hunting dogs due to their keen sense of smell. But she had always loved Aussies, so she decided to take a chance with Max. She was delighted to discover the breed's sense of smell was sharp enough to get the job done.

She climbed behind the wheel, pushed the shop door remote, then backed her pickup and enclosed trailer outside.

Ten minutes later, she pulled off to the side of the road and stopped. She grabbed her cellphone and punched Hailey's number. "I'm almost there."

"Okay. I'm heading out the door now. See you out front." Again Hailey hung up without saying goodbye.

Shelby pulled up in front of Hailey's A-frame home and saw her friend waiting on her covered porch.

Hailey loaded her bag in the back seat and hopped in. "Let's go." She tossed her long copper braid over her shoulder.

"Hello to you too," Shelby joked even though she knew when it came to a rescue, Hailey, an EMTI, was strung tighter than a high-wire at a circus.

Hailey had no more put her seat belt on before she turned her big blue eyes on Shelby and blurted, "How are you doing knowing that it's Ryker who's lost?"

Good question. Just how did she feel about seeing the man who still had power over her heart even though he had broken it into shards?

* * *

Thick snow swirled around Ryker Anderson to where he could barely see three-feet in front of him. He tried to start his snowmobile one more time, but it was dead. Poor Jeff and Scott and Adam. The three of them must be worried sick about him. He just hoped they didn't blame themselves for this. When the snow started falling, the four of them decided to head back to Jeff's truck in case the snow got worse. By the time they'd made the decision and were halfway there, the snowfall had increased and the visibility had decreased.

Easily the most experienced rider of the foursome, Ryker had come up the rear. Several times Jeff had looked back to make sure Ryker was behind him, and he had been too until his machine had died. When he finally got it running again, he tried to catch up with them, but the guys were nowhere in sight. Due to the heavy snowfall, Ryker wondered if he had gotten turned around without realizing it and had ridden in the wrong direction. If he had, and they had come back for him, they wouldn't know where to find him in this blizzard.

He unzipped the pocket inside his snow jacket and removed his GPS radio, a lifesaving must have for any snowmobiler. One glance at the blank screen, however, and he arched his head back and groaned. The batteries were dead. Earlier when he'd checked them, he had a feeling they might be low, but he ignored it because he always carried spares. Now, he could kick himself in the behind for not following his gut instinct.

He dug around in his backpack looking for his spare batteries. When he couldn't find them, he pulled everything out, and put everything back in one item at a time, making sure he hadn't overlooked them. Sure enough, they weren't there. Where were they? Earlier he had them when he'd double-checked his backpack by removing everything and putting it back before they left to go sledding. Unless...

When he was doing that, Jeff had asked him about Shelby and if Ryker had seen her since he'd gotten back. From that second on, his mind had been fixated on Shelby and nothing else.

He'd thought about her sweet disposition.

Her kind, caring, and compassionate heart.

The way her chocolate brown eyes lit up when she looked at him.

How her sandy-blonde bangs fell across one eye when she playfully pouted.

And her beautiful face and Barbie-doll lips. Lips he had kissed and had planned on kissing until the day he died, which according to his doctor should have already happened.

He closed his eyes, to blot back the tears of pain and regret. If only he knew now what he knew back then, he would have never made that phone call three months before their wedding to say goodbye to Shelby forever. Every day since then, that decision ate away at his heart and his conscience like a decomposing gangrene wound. But after the devastating news he'd received, his options had been limited. Ryker shook his head. He couldn't think about any of that now.

Couldn't think about how much he loved her.

How he'd never stopped loving her.

How much he missed her.

How his arms ached to hold her.

How sorry he was.

No, right now, he couldn't think of any of that. He needed to stay focused on staying alive so he could maybe, finally explain to Shelby why he had left. He owed her that much. Ryker only hoped she would give him that chance. Doubt crept in like an unwanted invader. She probably hated him, and he didn't blame her. Now that he looked back, he wished he could rewind his life and have a do over on how he had handled the whole situation.

His chest expanded as he drew in a weighty breath. Regrets and if onlys sure bogged a man's heart down. Well, enough regrets had consumed his life; he couldn't let the frigid elements consume it as well. He needed to get busy.

First mission, find some dry wood to start a fire with. Everything he found though was either too wet or too green so there would be no warm fire tonight. Now what?

He still had a hard time wrapping his mind around the fact that he was lost. Having been born and raised here, every winter, he had snowmobiled this area, and every summer he had hiked here. He knew every inch of Gravel Mountain like the back of his hand, so how could he possibly have gotten lost? Probably the same way everyone else who knew every inch of this mountain did. Blizzards had a way of making that happen, especially without a GPS to guide you. Even so, it had never happened to him before. Until now.

To make matters worse, his friend Jeff had his cellphone. Around eleven, when the guys wanted to stop for lunch, because Jeff's replacement phone hadn't arrived, Jeff had borrowed Ryker's to cancel a meeting he'd forgotten to cancel. Ryker gave it to him and then started riding again, and he had forgotten to get it back. That seemed to be his luck every time any thought of Shelby brushed by. Why did he lose his mind and good senses when her name came up or her face flitted into his thoughts?

Knowing there was nothing he could do about any of those things now, he got back to work, trying everything he knew to keep himself alive.

Each breath and movement became a slow slogging effort, and when he'd finally eliminated all his options but one, he grabbed his shovel and got busy building a snow cave. Finished and deathly tired, he hunkered down inside the makeshift hollow and huddled up. His thoughts traipsed here and there, alighting on things he hadn't thought of in years. Knowing he needed to stay focused, he did what came natural to him.

Whenever he found himself in trouble or needing comfort, he always quoted God's Word. *"Be merciful, to me, oh God, be merciful to me! For my soul trusts in You; and in the shadow of Your wings I will make my refuge, until these calamities have passed by. The name of the Lord is a strong tower. The righteous run to it and are safe.* Thank You, Father, for these promises in Psalm 57:1 and Proverbs 18:10. They're my hope and my comfort right now. No, *You're* my hope and comfort.

"Send Your angels to watch over me, Lord, and keep me safe. And please keep me alive and give me a chance explain to Shelby why I left. I can't stand the thought of her not knowing the truth. That it had nothing to do with her. That it had everything to do with me dying." Strange that now, after all this time, he might be prevented from telling her he left because he was dying by him actually dying. Could life really be that cruel?

Cold seeped through his many layers of clothing and into his body. If someone didn't find him soon, he wouldn't get the chance to tell Shelby anything, and on that thought, he began to drift away.

Chapter Two

Shelby and Hailey trekked their way through the deep snow to the command center that was set up inside a spacious enclosed snowmobile trailer heated by a large generator. Just steps before it, Shelby noticed a familiar tall, stocky figure. "Jeff? Jeff Bower? Is that you?" Puffs of white floated through the frigid air as she spoke.

"Shelby!" One yank and she found herself in Jeff's arms. He held onto her so tight, she could hardly breathe. Relief brushed through her when he finally let her go.

"What are you doing here?" Shelby asked him, bewildered by his reaction to her.

"It's all my fault, Shelby." Jeff shook his head.

"What's all your fault?"

"One minute we were all together and the next." He pinched his eyes shut and shrugged. "We went back, but we couldn't find him. We decided the best thing to do was to get back to the truck and radio for help. I mean, what good would it do if we were all lost and in different directions, right?" He shoved his hands into his snow pants. "I should have looked back. I thought Ryker was with the rest of us. I didn't know." He shook his head, his shoulders hunkered forward, dejection masked his face and moisture sheened his hazel eyes.

"Don't blame yourself, Jeff." Shelby put her arm around him. "These things happen, more than you know.

He'll be okay. Ryker's a survivor. We'll find him."

"How? I still have his cellphone. I forgot to give it back to him. And," his head dropped, and he weaved it back and forth. "I should have never asked him about you." Wide apologetic eyes yanked up to hers before he quickly looked away.

Shelby wondered what Ryker had to say about her, but she refused to ask. Now was not the time for that.

"I guess we both were so distracted that neither one of us noticed when he was putting everything back into his backpack that his batteries had fallen out and had gotten kicked under the truck. I found them when we got back. Oh man." Jeff covered his eyes with his large hand. "If I hadn't distracted him and hadn't forgotten to give Ryker his cellphone then... If anything happens to him..." His voice cracked, and the comment hung between them.

Shelby wanted to comfort Jeff, but Hailey strode toward her, and time was a wasting. They had to find Ryker, and quick.

"Shelby, everyone's here," Hailey said from behind Jeff.

"Be right there." She gave Jeff another hug. "You need to get inside where it's warm, okay? Don't worry. We'll find Ryker. I promise."

He nodded. His faith in her blessed her. She only hoped she didn't let him down, that she could keep that promise. For more reasons than one.

Once inside the trailer, everyone gathered and their team leader took charge. Laminated maps hung on the wall, and a perimeter had already been circled where

Ryker had last been seen. Any possible exits were circled also. The goal - to corral Ryker, if possible. The team leader organized them into teams of four and said once they reached the scene point, the last place Ryker had been seen, they would split. It was all protocol, but the rules were necessary to repeat so everyone operated on the same instructions.

When the leader finished, everyone made sure their communication devices and other transmitters were all working properly. Then they all dressed in their warmest snowmobile garb. Shelby, Devin, Hailey and Tim were on the same team. They unloaded the machines from their trailers and gathered all the gear they would need. When they finished, Shelby settled Max in the special box she'd had custom-made on the back of her snowmobile to make sure her dog wasn't anywhere near the sled's exhaust so his sense of smell wouldn't be hindered from finding a scent.

All the search and rescue members headed out. Three members, Shelby, and her dog headed to the last scene point. Some teams headed for the drainage in front of Ryker to where they could search backward toward the last scene point. Those team members would do a visual search while Shelby worked her dog off the last scene point.

Following her GPS's coordinates, she took the lead, and all four of them headed in the direction they were given. Fresh powdered snow sprayed from their sleds as they weaved through the pine and aspen trees and across the clearings.

The only light they had to guide them came from the

ones on their snowmobiles and their headlamps.

They finally arrived at the last scene point on Gravel Mountain. Shelby, the dog handler in this search and rescue, along with Tim, her support member, took off from the last scene point and the other two went up higher to begin a visual search on a higher elevation.

Two hours into the search, mixed emotions flooded Shelby. It had finally stopped snowing. For that she was elated, but at the same time it bothered her because a clear sky meant an even further drop in temperatures and therefore an even lower probability of finding Ryker alive, especially if they didn't get to him soon. That is, if he was even still alive now. Shelby banished those heart-shattering thoughts from her brain. She couldn't think that way. She had to stay focused. Ryker's life depended on it.

The whole time they searched, Shelby prayed that God would let them find him alive. No matter how deeply he had hurt her, she wished her ex-fiancé no harm. After all, she still loved him even though she didn't trust him any further than she could toss him, which wasn't far. Ryker was a six-foot-two, stocky, muscle-clad, six-pack-abs toting man. Tossing him with anything other than her heart would have been impossible.

Hours later, around one in the morning, Shelby spotted what looked like a snowmobile glinting in the moonlight in the distance. When she came up on the machine, she glanced around.

No Ryker.

Dear God, no!

Tears stung the back of her eyes, but there was no time for crying, so she forced them back. She needed to keep her wits about her.

Tim pulled his sled alongside hers and turned it off. She reached over and turned the key shutting hers down too. He must have sensed her fear and uncertainty because he reached for her hand and gave it a squeeze. "Don't give up, Shelby. We'll find him." Tim's voice held nothing but compassion.

Shelby nodded, praying Tim was right.

They both dismounted. She held onto Max's leash while she and Tim did a 360 of the area, looking for any signs or tracks or clothing. They searched the snowmobile for a backpack or any article of clothing or something Shelby could use as a scent-smell so that Max could find Ryker, but they came up empty. Not one item at all. Giving up was not an option. There had to be something. *Lord, we could sure use Your help here. We need something, anything to help track Ryker.*

"Over here," Tim hollered, his voice echoed through the darkness and trees.

Shelby and Max rushed to where Tim stood amidst a cluster of aspen trees.

"This looks like a shirttail someone's torn off." Tim raised his helmet and smelled the cloth. "Pew." He jerked it away, wrinkling his nose. "We can't use this. It smells like fuel." He tossed it far away from them.

Shelby looked around. "There's some tracks. They're heading up that way." She pointed to another cluster of trees. Amidst the trees she found a trail mix wrapper and picked it up. "Maybe this will help us."

Shelby placed the crinkly paper under Max's nose. Max sniffed the ground where the tracks were. Suddenly, he took off, and Shelby held on to his leash with every bit of strength she had. His aggressiveness was a sure sign they were near.

Her pulse quickened as she followed her dog around trees and over logs.

She wanted to let Max go, but if Ryker suffered from hypothermia, they would have to approach him gently, otherwise if they startled him he could go into cardiac arrest and die.

Die. That one word knifed through her with an ache so deep she didn't know how she could even breathe.

Using all her willpower to restrain her leader, she held on tight while Max all but dragged her to what appeared to be a makeshift snow cave. Max ducked his head inside. His tail wagged furiously, another sign he'd found who they were searching for. Shelby pulled back on his leash, got on her knees, and peered inside. Hunkered inside, dressed in all his snowmobile garb, Ryker sat on his backpack with his ankles crossed, and his eyes closed, oblivious to her presence. Not a good sign.

Not a good sign at all.

Shelby swallowed the rising lump of fear in her throat. Seeing him for the first time since he'd left her was like seeing a ghost, a mirage, but this was no mirage and no ghost. This was real. More real than she wanted it to be, especially under these wretched circumstances.

Her emotions played tug-of-war with her heart, and her arms ached to hold him, to tell him everything was going to be okay. That she was here. But, she couldn't. No, she wouldn't. He didn't belong to her anymore and never would.

She inhaled a long, scalding breath of frigid air in hopes of getting her emotions under control and prayed for God to give her the strength she needed to endure this.

Kneeling all the way into the snow, she showed Max her gratitude for finding Ryker. "Good boy, Max." She rewarded her dog for finding Ryker, then extended Max's leash toward Tim.

It was time to take charge. "Hold Max for me, please."

Tim took the leash from her.

"And would you go get my gear for me?" Before she got her question out, Tim had already turned and headed the direction of their sleds.

Shelby got on her hands and knees and crawled inside the small snow cave. Once she assessed Ryker's medical condition, she backed out. Moving as quickly as she could, she checked her GPS, and called the command center. She reported the missing person found, gave them their coordinates, described Ryker as a two, which meant he needed medical assistance, then walked through the medical with them. Shelby sighed long and hard, relieved that Ryker wasn't a three, which meant he was already gone. A one would have been better, but that wasn't the case. Ryker needed help, and he needed it ASAP.

In order not to startle Ryker, she moved cautiously and with great care around the perimeter of the cave.

Tim arrived with their gear, huffing and puffing his way up to her with Max lunging forward through the deep snow at his side.

"Sit, Max. Stay." Her dog immediately obeyed. "You can drop his leash now."

She and Tim, a friend of her parents, had worked together many times before. They both knew what to do.

While she grabbed the life bag, an insulated sleeping bag with reflective thermal lining, Tim grabbed the mountain stove he carried in his backpack.

Lord, help me not to startle him. You know if I do that his heart could start beating so fast that he could go into cardiac arrest. Please, help me and please keep Ryker safe. Don't let him d— No! He can't die. Please, Lord.

She crawled inside the snow cave and in a soft gentle tone, she said, "Ryker, this is Shelby." For a brief second she waited for a reaction. None came. Once again she swallowed back her fear. "I'm here to help you, Ryker. I'm going to put a sleeping bag on you now to help warm you up." As gently as she could, she covered his body with the bag. He moaned, and Shelby's motion stopped. Although she'd done this forty or fifty times since becoming a certified dog trainer and handler, this time was different.

So as not to make a mistake, she mentally went through the steps in her mind.

One: Due to the lack of blood flow to his extremities be careful and move with kid gloves.

Two: Warm Ryker slowly and carefully.

Three: Don't rush to bring him around. Go slow by

giving him sips of water and by talking to him.

Feeling a bit more confident and stable, Shelby pulled out one of the bottles of water she kept near her body in order to keep it warm, and laid it against Ryker's lips. Firm yet soft lips that once kissed her with a love unlike anything she had ever known before or since. *Shelby, stop it. You're a professional. Now is not the time to be thinking about that. Besides, you need to remember that he dumped you.* That last thought gave her all the incentive she needed to once again remember why she was here and to detach from any sentimental feelings that tried to slither into her consciousness.

It was a good thing too because it was unsafe to move him until they had him stabilized, and that meant she would be hunkered in here with him until daylight. Come morning, she would take him to an awaiting Evac chopper or ambulance. Once she handed him over safely, then she never had to give Ryker Anderson another thought or ever see his handsome face again. Her attention slid to Ryker. Morning couldn't come soon enough.

Chapter Three

"Ryker, can you hear me?" Through an obscure, distant fog, Ryker heard what sounded like Shelby's voice. But that couldn't be. Shelby was long gone, only a memory. Perhaps it was because he felt so close to death that it was wishful thinking on his part. Either that or he really was hallucinating. If only he could get his brain to work right. But even in his wildest drinking days, he hadn't been this hallucinogenic. It all seemed incredibly real, like he could reach out and actually touch her.

Warm liquid slid down his throat. He coughed it back, surprised at the onslaught.

"Ryker? Can you hear me?" There it was again. That sweet, gentle voice that sounded so much like Shelby's.

Shelby? Was she really here?

Or was it all an illusion?

The thought slip-slid through his mind, finding traction only to lose its footing again.

No. It couldn't be her. She hated him.

He had to be hallucinating. There was no other explanation. Or was there?

The question and need to know lingered in his brain like a heavy fog. He tried to open his eyes, but they were heavy and refused to open to the world.

"Ryker, come on. Open your eyes, please."

That raspy tone sure sounded like Shelby's.

With everything inside Ryker, he struggled to raise his eyelids, to see if it really was her or if his mind was making this all up. Through a slit in his eyes, an apparition of Shelby appeared in front of them distorted and hazy.

Was she really here?

He didn't know, couldn't tell.

So confused.

So tired.

And so cold.

"He's waking up."

Wait. Whose voice was that? Not Shelby's. Too deep. Like a man's.

Or was he hearing things? He tried to turn his head to get a reading on who else might be there, but the effort left him even more exhausted.

What was going on? His body felt numb, almost out of his control.

He struggled to make sense of things, but nothing made any sense at all. He forced his tongue to work. "Sh—Sh—Shelby," he rasped through chattering teeth. "Ith—Ith tha' you?"

"Yes, Ryker, it's me."

Her words and face blended together so seamlessly he began to believe he wasn't hallucinating and that she really was here.

But why?

His brain scrambled to remember where he was. Maybe if he could figure that out, he could find an answer as to why Shelby would be here.

"I'm so glad we found him." There was that deep male voice again. It sounded vaguely familiar.

Just what did he mean by 'we found him'?

Had he been lost?

What was going on?

Confusion swirled inside his head so he couldn't tell what was reality and what wasn't.

A chill skittered down his spine. "Ahm-ahm so-so ca-ca-cold." Exhaustion peeled the last layer of his determination away, and his vision went black as his already half-mast eyes drifted shut.

Something hard settled gently against his lips and more tepid liquid slid down his throat.

"Ryker, open your eyes." There was that raspy tone again, but now they held a demand and a plea in them.

He summoned strength back to him. In slow motion, his eyelids rose until those same brown eyes he'd been dreaming about for months were now directly in front of him, staring at him, and filled with worry. "Wha—wha' ar—ar- you—you doin' ha—here?" His words were broken and barely audible even to his own ears.

"I'm here to help you. To take you back."

Take him back? Did that mean that she had forgiven him?

"We can't take you anywhere right now though. We'll have to wait until daylight. Right now, we need to get you warmed up and stable."

Stable? The word did the slip-sliding thing through his brain again.

No matter how hard he tried to make sense of

things, very little came together. What little he could decipher came in bits and pieces. One thing that did make sense to him, the one thing he fully understood was... he was chilled to the bone and needed something to warm him up. Whatever covered his body felt nice and helped, but not nearly enough. "Whe—where am I?"

"Don't you remember what happened?" Shelby's gentle question had his mind clambering for the answer.

"No." His head weaved back and forth, but he stopped it because the motion hurt too much. "No, I—I don't." Frustrated about what was going on with him, he pinched his eyes shut and tried desperately to remember something. Anything. But the effort was too much, and his body slumped.

A gentle hand lifted his head. "Don't worry about trying to remember, Ryker. It's okay." Shelby continued to give him water and continued to talk to him.

"My arms and legs are tingling like crazy." His mind had started to clear. Slowly bits and pieces were coming back to him now. He'd been snowmobiling with his buddies.

There was a storm.

His machine had died.

Couldn't get it started.

No phone.

No replacement batteries for his GPS.

Building a snow cave.

His last thoughts were of Shelby.

He dragged his focus onto her. God had answered his prayer. The Lord had given him an opportunity to explain why he had broken off their engagement. *Thank you, Lord.* "Shelby, can we talk?"

* * *

Shelby stiffened. He probably wanted to explain to her why he'd abandoned her. Well, she didn't want to hear any of his excuses or his reasons for why he'd done it. As far as she was concerned nothing he had to say would make up for his leaving her like he had. Therefore she had no desire whatsoever to talk to him about that or anything else.

Not now.

Not later.

Not ever.

"Tim, would you take over here." She handed Tim the water bottle. "I need to step outside and inform the command center that we're ready to transport Ryker out of here." One quick glance at Ryker and the hurt in his blue eyes, and she skedaddled out of the shelter as fast as she could.

Shelby battled to not be moved by the hurt and disappointment in Ryker's eyes. Having her heart battered by him once already was enough. A second time, she closed her eyes and shook her head, there was no way she could endure that kind of torture ever again.

When she finished contacting the command center, she decided not to go back inside the snow cave even though it was warmer in there with the mountain stove running. Instead, she paced outside, waiting until the other search and rescue members arrived to help her and Tim transfer Ryker. Shelby glanced at the time on her

GPS. It had been four and half hours since they'd found Ryker. Barely twilight outside, there was enough light to safely transport Ryker to the awaiting ambulance. She couldn't wait. Her heart couldn't take much more.

Snowmobile sounds echoed through the trees, snagging Shelby's attention. Help had finally arrived. Her eyes darted upward. "Thank you, Lord."

Hailey and two other men came into view. One man sat on the back of Hailey's snowmobile, and the other drove one with a rescue sled hooked behind it.

Hailey introduced the two men quickly, and Shelby led them to the snow cave. On her way there, Hailey hooked her arm through Shelby's. "How's Ryker?"

"Better now."

"That's good. I was afraid we'd be too late." Hailey stumbled, and Shelby steadied her. "So how are *you* doing?"

The question sliced through Shelby's carefully woven shield of an in control professional just doing her job. "Don't ask."

"That bad, huh?"

"Let's just say I've had better days. Much, much better."

They reached the snow cave, and the group worked together to prep Ryker for his ride back to the ambulance, each one working their part like a well-timed machine.

Finally, it was time to head out. Shelby walked around her sled and the transport where Ryker lay strapped just to make sure everything was indeed secure.

"Shelby."

She wanted to keep walking, to pretend she hadn't heard him, but she couldn't be cold-hearted like that. Worse, her heart jerked her gaze down to Ryker lying flat on the rescue sled all bundled up. And then as if they were being led by a greater force than her own will, her eyes had the nerve to snag onto his.

"Will you ride with me?"

Anger. Hurt. Insanity poured into her. Was he kidding? Didn't he know what he had done to her? Her gaze raked over him, and her heart went into fits and starts. Seeing him lying there looking so helpless, like a small, pleading child, her heart softened. How could she say no? Wait! What was she thinking? She didn't dare give into him and that vulnerable way he was looking at her. He'd only hurt her again if she did. She wrenched her focus off of him and yanked it over onto Hailey and Tim.

Two sympathetic faces stared back at her. Hailey and Tim were the only two rescue members here who knew of her past with Ryker. The other two helpers Hugh and Jace didn't.

Without looking at Ryker again for fear she would give into him despite her self-talk against it, she said, "I can't. Hailey is an EMTI, and she has to ride with you so she can monitor you. Tim will be standing on the back of the sled, and Hugh and Jace will be driving the other machines out. That leaves me to drive you out with mine."

Before she could hear his reply, Shelby slid in front of Max already seated in the box seat on her sled waiting for her. To drown out anything else Ryker might say, she fired up her machine.

The long slow ride down to the awaiting ambulance was the longest ride of her life. Memories—near ones and far—played through her mind relentlessly until she thought she would go mad.

Like the times when she and Ryker had walked the sandy shores of Grand Lake in their bare feet, holding hands, and talking about their future together.

Times of shared kisses on the pontoon boat when the full moon sent its orange and yellow glow dancing across the glassy surface of the lake.

Hugs and whispers of I love you.

Those words, those images, continued to haunt her as her snowmobile glided across the snow with Ryker on the rescue sled hooked to her machine.

Ryker within reach, yet inaccessible.

The pain of his abandonment hit her full force. She couldn't wait to get back to the command center, load everything up, and go home.

To put all this behind her.

To put Ryker behind her.

Again.

Her mind and her heart screamed in protest. All of that was going to be far easier said than done.

Why? Why did it have to be Ryker that needed rescuing? Seeing him again had resurrected all those old feelings she had struggled to bury for so long. Not just the feelings of anger she had toward him for abandoning her, but the feelings of love that had stayed nestled in her heart no matter how many times over the last eighteen months she had tried to pluck them out. Love now frightened her in ways it never had before.

It held too much power.

Too much control.

Too much pain.

Never again would she trust someone with her heart.

Especially not Ryker.

Chapter Four

As time slid forward, Ryker realized he would survive his bout with hypothermia. Even better in a strange way, he was going to live, but after getting the brush off that he deserved from Shelby, he wasn't at all sure that he wanted to. He was supposed to be dead by now anyway.

He'd now survived two days in the hospital without one word from Shelby. The last time he'd seen her was when she handed him over to the ambulance crew at the bottom of the mountain. Not that he expected to hear from her. It was only wishful thinking on his part.

Inside that snow cave up on the mountain, seeing Shelby for the first time since discovering his diagnosis all those long days before, had been sheer torture. It was if someone had taken a buoy knife and stabbed it into his heart, plunging it deeper and deeper with each word, each touch.

Is that how Shelby had felt eighteen months ago? A fresh onslaught of pain attacked him for what Shelby must have gone through. For what he had put her through. If only he could tell her that he'd done it *for* her, not *to* her, to spare her the grief of watching him die a slow painful death, and to keep from bringing a child into the world only to leave that little one fatherless.

Ryker turned over, the thoughts refusing to leave

him alone. He knew just how hard something like that was to go through. Two guys he went to high school with grew up without dads. Numerous times they had told Ryker how envious they were of him because he had a dad to come and watch him play football, to go fishing with, and to do things with. Many times, in their weak moments, they'd cried and poured their hearts out to Ryker. He never forgot how much they went through by not having a father and how desperately they craved a father's love.

Then, like a slow-motion horror film, he'd watched his older brother Randy slowly waste away from the cancer that ravaged his body. Seeing the brother he loved so very much, looked up to, and adored, writhe with pain that no pain killer could relieve. The agony of watching his brother dying as he looked on completely helpless had been almost more than Ryker could bear. Never, ever had he felt so hopeless or so useless in his whole life. It was the worst thing he'd ever endured, next to saying goodbye to Shelby. But he had to. He didn't want that same torment for Shelby, so at the time he did what he believed was best for her.

Emotionally and physically drained from the memories that simply wouldn't go away, Ryker closed his eyes.

For the hundredth time since arriving at the hospital, her face popped into his mind and stuck there.

To blot out the image, he opened his eyes, hoping her face wouldn't be there too. Her face wasn't, but her presence was. Not physically, but emotionally. Everything he did and thought about came back to

Shelby. It did no good to torment himself with a longing that would probably never be filled, unless she forgave him. And his chances of that were as slim as him getting out of here in the next thirty seconds.

It was his own fault. He should have told her why he was leaving instead of just calling her and saying goodbye. But he had to. Otherwise she would have talked him into still marrying her regardless of his dying. Well, it would be a hot day in Iceland before he would have done that to her. The whole thing was a no-win situation.

"Good evening, Mr. Anderson. I brought you some flowers." Jennifer, the brown-haired, green-eyed nurse who'd taken care of him all day, the very one who would make even an energizer battery nervous, came bouncing into his room, holding a huge bouquet of flowers.

"Thank you, Jennifer. Just put them over there with the rest of the balloons and flowers."

"Don't you even want to see who they're from?" Her pencil-thin eyebrows rose.

Guilt nipped at his conscience. The only person he genuinely cared about sending him flowers was Shelby, and he knew they weren't from her. Still, shame on him. Someone had gone through the trouble to send him some, and he should be grateful they had thought enough about him to do that. *Sorry, Lord. Forgive me.* "Sure."

Jennifer set them on the portable hospital table and wheeled it closer to him.

"Thank you."

"You're welcome," she chirped, her smile warm and friendly. A cute little gal to be sure, but she wasn't

Shelby. "Can I get you anything else?"

Shelby, he wanted to say, but no one could give him Shelby except for Shelby herself. "No, thank you."

"If you need anything, just press the button." Jennifer repeated for the thirtieth time in twelve hours. She excused herself and left the same way she had come in as if she had springs on her feet. Tigger, the tiger from Winnie the Pooh, his bounce was nothing next to hers.

Shelby had a lot of energy too but nothing compared to Jennifer's. Truth was, he preferred Shelby's energetic ways. Oh man. Why did every thought keep coming back around to Shelby? He needed to stop thinking about her. His heart couldn't take much more of this.

But that was easier said than done. Especially when Shelby's favorite flowers, delphiniums, light-blue irises, and hydrangeas, all her favorite color, were staring him in the face.

He plucked the card from the little, pitch-fork-looking thing sticking out of the flowers, and opened the card.

Glad to hear you're doing better.
Shelby.

Shelby. He couldn't believe it. Nor did he dare let himself hope this meant anything. Still, a smile hid behind his heart that it just might. A guy could always hope, especially when hope was all he had left.

* * *

Sitting at the computer desk in her office, Shelby shoved her comfy leather chair across the knotty-pine floor toward the large picture window overlooking Grand Lake, and crossed her legs. Her foot jiggled as she stared into the yellow, orange-tipped flames of her gas fireplace. "Stupid, stupid, stupid. What was I thinking?"

Max rose from his dog bed and shoved his head under her hand. She leaned over and kissed the top of his furry head. One blue eye and one brown eye stared up at her. "Don't ever fall in love, Max. It hurts too much. And don't ever do anything stupid like I just did." Max licked her hand, and Shelby ruffled his ears. "Why did I send those flowers? I should be strong. Strong. Go on with my life. Quit thinking about him."

Shelby wanted to rush to the hospital and try to catch the delivery person before they gave Ryker the flowers she'd ordered in one of her weakest moments. Surely that had to be why she'd done it for there could be no other reason.

"Argggh." Her office chair rolled across the room when she stood abruptly. She walked around the side of her desk that faced the double sliding glass doors. She crossed her arms and leaned one shoulder against the cool glass pane wishing she would have never sent Ryker those flowers. True, she tried to make the note simple. But what if he got the wrong idea? What if he thought she'd forgiven him or something equally as crazy like she was befriending him or something?

Really, all she had wanted to do was be kind to a man who had almost died. Even if that man was her ex-fiancé. Despite what he'd done to her, she truly was glad he was doing better. Just as she would be if any other fellow human being who'd gone through what he had survived. And if she thought that way long enough she just might believe it herself. Pushing her fingers through her blonde bangs, she sighed to the core of her soul.

"Who are you kidding? You've never stopped loving him." That was true enough. She had never really stopped loving him, but it still didn't change the fact that she could never trust her heart to him again even though a part of her longed to do that very thing.

Ever since the moment she had found out it was Ryker who was lost, she'd struggled to get her emotions under control, and it was becoming painfully obvious they were getting farther and farther out of her control.

For the very life of her, she just couldn't understand how a person could love someone so deeply and yet hate them at the same time.

Hate was a mighty powerful word. Every bit as powerful as love. Both seemed destined to rip her apart.

For the millionth time she asked herself if she really hated Ryker, or if she just hated what he'd done to her?

A long drawn-out sigh slid out of her. The truth was she didn't hate anyone, including Ryker. What he did to her, she hated, but wishing him ill or condemning him, no.

She shoved away from the window. Why was she even thinking about all of this anyway? She should just do what all of her friends had told her to do the first twelve months after Ryker had disappeared—-forget about him and go on with her life.

Eighteen months, and a million aches later, she thought she had finally succeeded in doing just that. But now he was back, and she was right back where she'd started. For her own sanity, she had to figure out a way to put Ryker far from her thoughts so she could get on with her life.

Determination to do that very thing rose up in her. She strode over to her office chair and pulled it in front of her computer. Double-clicking her Word document, she positioned her fingers, tapping lightly on the keys while she waited for the blank document to open. As soon as it did, she began to type.

Chapter One

Cherri Lauer's heart stopped the second she heard the mention of his name. What was he doing back in town? He wasn't welcome here anymore. Still, Stryker was in danger and he needed her.

Shelby's fingers froze above the keys.

"Stryker? Seriously, Shelby? You named your hero Stryker? As in Ryker?" The question hung in the air.

Ack! So much for getting her mind off of Ryker.

She flopped her head against the headrest of her office chair. Her arms dropped to her side, hanging there like a ragdoll's, and her gaze darted toward the ceiling and held there.

Why did she have to see him again?

Why did her heart go all agog thinking about him?

Why did she have to still love him even after what he'd done?

And would her thoughts and her heart *ever* be free from Ryker?

Did she even want them to?

God have mercy on me. I still love him. I can't help myself. But I can never trust him again. Please show me what to do.

The words *Forgive him* slipped into her spirit.

Shelby bolted upright in her chair. "You've got to be kidding me, Lord. What he did was inexcusable. Nothing short of death could ever be a good enough reason to leave like that. I'm sorry, Lord, but I can never forgive him. Never!"

Days later, Shelby sat at her breakfast nook, sipping on her cappuccino. She tossed the last piece of buttered wheat toast into her mouth. If she didn't hurry, she'd be late for church, so she quickly put on her boots, coat and gloves. A quick pat to her pocket told her what she needed to know. Her pocket-size Bible was safely tucked inside.

For today's potluck, she'd made a crockpot full of chili. She unplugged the crockpot, gathered the freshly-baked cornbread and softened butter, placed them all on top of a blanket-lined crate, and folded the ends of the blanket over the items. She hoisted the box up and headed toward the front door.

Outdoors, it was another typical December day in Grand Lake.

The sun shone brightly, but no heat accompanied it. She shivered from the cold tracing through her body.

Crusted snow topped with three inches of fresh white powder crunched under her feet.

Today she'd drive her SUV instead of her truck. Taking time to unhitch the trailer would make her late for church.

Minutes later, the log church building near the lake came into view. She parked her vehicle out front, went around the passenger side door and grabbed her contribution to today's luncheon, and headed inside where it was warm.

Mrs. McIntyre with her grayish-blue, bobbed style hairdo greeted Shelby the instant she stepped inside the large foyer and closed the door. "Good morning, Sugar."

"Good morning, Mrs. McIntyre." Shelby shifted the heavy box.

"Lawrence, come take this box and put it downstairs in the kitchen."

Shelby reshifted her burden. "Oh, no, that's okay. I can get it."

"Nonsense. Lawrence can do it. He knows where I want everything, don't you, sweetie?" Love and admiration shown in both of the older couple's eyes.

How Shelby wished she had a love like that. She had at one time. Not wanting to go down that well-traveled road, she mentally rattled that thought right out of her mind as she handed the box over to Mr. McIntyre. "The crockpot needs to be plugged in, okay?"

"Don't you worry none. I'll take care of everything."

"Thank you."

He headed toward the basement stairs and disappeared out of sight.

Shelby turned her attention back to Mrs. McIntyre. "I really could have taken that downstairs myself."

"He loves doing it. Besides the exercise is good for his heart. Speaking of heart, how's your dad doing? Is he getting any better?"

"Yes, he's feeling much better. He's started

exercising regularly and has lost over sixty pounds. His blood pressure is back to normal now, and the doctors have given him a clean bill of health. Well, except for his asthma. They're coming up here sometime this week to spend the holidays with me."

"Oh, that's so nice to hear." Her hazel eyes sparkled. "I sure do miss your mother. I wish they wouldn't have moved down the mountain. Denver's such a busy place. Why anyone would want to move down there with all that traffic and noise and smog," she wrinkled her nose and fanned her face, "is beyond me. Give me snow, cold and fresh air any old day."

"Me too." Since no one else had arrived yet except for the band members and a few others who were already seated, Shelby took a minute to invite Mr. and Mrs. McIntyre to join her and her parents for dinner Friday night.

"We'd love to come, wouldn't we, sweetie?"

Shelby turned around to find Mr. McIntyre standing behind her.

"We sure would. You still got that old Monopoly game?"

"Sure do."

"Well, get it ready, because this time I'm going to beat that dad of yours."

Shelby laughed. Poor Mr. McIntyre had been trying for years to beat her dad at Monopoly and had yet to succeed. She secretly hoped this time he would, for his sake.

One of the large wooden double-doors, opened and a small gaggle of tourists stepped inside, stomping the snow from their boots and wiping their feet on the burgundy throw rug.

Shelby gave Mrs. McIntyre a quick hug and headed into the sanctuary.

After hugging and greeting those she knew, she hurried to her usual seat in the back and sat down on the padded pew.

She liked sitting in the back row and observing people. Grand Lake was such a big tourist town and all sorts of folks came here from all over the world. Observing them made great fodder for her novels.

Several of the locals greeted her as they headed toward their seats, and she greeted a passel of visitors and welcomed them to church.

As the worship band picked up their instruments, Todd, the worship leader, pulled the microphone closer to him. "Good morning, everyone. Welcome to Shadow Mountain Fellowship. It's nice to see so many new faces here. It always blesses me to see people who have come here on vacation or who are here visiting take the time to come and worship our Lord. We're so glad you joined us today. Thank you for coming. And now, if you would all stand, we'll get started."

When Todd and the band started playing and singing, Shelby closed her eyes and let the words wash over as she focused on God. Praise rose from her heart and whispered through her lips.

Feeling God's presence permeate the room sent liquid love bathing over her. She wanted to stay in His presence forever. But all too soon worship was over.

The band members placed their instruments where

they normally kept them, and Pastor Nigel Roberts stepped up to the glass podium. "Good morning, everyone. As always, it's a pleasure to see so many new faces here this morning. And familiar ones too." Nigel smiled.

Shelby loved this church and her church family. They didn't just talk the talk, they walked the walk. Their goal was to crowd heaven with souls and to help as many people as they possibly could in this life.

A late comer slid in beside her.

She turned to welcome the person, but the smile and words froze on her lips, and her eyes narrowed. "What are you doing here?" she whispered.

"The same thing as you. I came to worship and to hear the word of God." Ryker's smile sent ice through her veins.

"Well, there are other places in here to sit, you know?"

"I do." His smile stayed in place.

Shelby wanted to wipe that smile off of his handsome face, but instead she gave him a well-then-do-it-already-look.

However, instead of taking the hint, he turned his face toward the front of the church.

Seriously? Shelby rolled her eyes and scooted over as far as she could, which wasn't very far because if she moved over any more she would end up sitting on the old man's lap next to her.

She folded her arms like a pretzel and settled them across her chest, full well knowing she was acting childish. But just who did Ryker think he was anyway showing up here at *her* church and disrupting her life like this after dumping her?

This isn't your church, Shelby, it's Mine.

The Holy Spirit was right, so she quickly repented for thinking this was her church. This was God's house and any and all were welcome, including Ryker. Still, did he have to sit right next to her? Couldn't he sit across the aisle? There was room on the bench over there or across the church. That would be even better. Then it occurred to her that she could go over there and sit.

No sooner had that thought come when a couple slipped into that spot and a family came to take the other.

The only other empty place was up front, and she wasn't going to make a spectacle of herself by going up there. No, she was stuck. But she didn't have to like it.

Her arms unwound, and with immense determination, she settled her hands on her lap. She tried to focus on what Nigel was saying, but her thoughts kept trailing to the man only inches from her.

The man who smelled of citrus pine and cool crisp air.

The very one she loved and despised at the same time.

Out of the corner of her eye, she watched him, completely engrossed in Nigel's sermon. And... completely ignoring her.

Well, isn't that what you wanted, Shelby? Or was it?

Ack! She didn't know anymore, and she hated that.

* * *

Ryker had a hard time concentrating on the pastor's sermon. He berated himself for not honoring Shelby's wish to sit somewhere else. Now it was too late. All the other spots were taken in the back, and he wasn't going to disrupt the service and go up front. He should have never sat by her in the first place. He had no right, he knew that, but he refused to give up. If only she'd let him explain why he had left her.

"Take the hand of the person next to you and let's pray."

Ryker didn't know whether to take Shelby's hand or not. Then, the decision was made. Without looking he let his hand search for hers. When his brushed against hers, she yanked it out of the way. Not one to give up so easily, he boldly found her hand and gathered it into his. Like it always had in the past, her hand fit nicely right there. Only this time there was no warmth in the connection, only a stiffness and a disconnect he couldn't deny. Still he would relish this opportunity to touch her.

When the prayer ended with a blessing over the food, Shelby tugged her hand out of his. Ryker wanted to snatch it back, to walk out of the church with her by his side, but he'd lost that privilege and that right when he'd said goodbye to her.

Pastor Roberts finished with an invitation to everyone to join them downstairs for their monthly pot-blessing as he called it instead of pot-luck. He said he didn't believe in luck. Ryker wasn't so sure he did anymore either, especially after the cold shoulder treatment Shelby gave him during the whole service.

What did you expect? That she would huddle up next

to you and hold your hand and rest her head on your shoulder like she used to? Well, face it, buddy. It's going to take a lot of work and a lot of patience and a ton of prayers to try and win her back. All of which he was more than willing to do. He only hoped she would give him a sliver of hope that his efforts wouldn't be completely futile.

He slipped out into the aisle and into the foyer. Several people he knew came up to him and hugged him. The whole time they did, he struggled to keep his eye on Shelby. But being completely surrounded now, he lost track of her.

"You're going to join us downstairs, aren't you?" Tyler Williams, the man whose snowmobile shop he'd just purchased, asked.

"Of course he is," Arlana, Tyler's wife, answered for him. The woman barely came up to Ryker's chest. Her auburn hair and pixie face made her look like she was in her mid-twenties instead of her mid-fifties.

Arlana hooked her arms through both Ryker's and Tyler's and led them toward the stairs. Only when they reached the stairwell did she let go.

The smell of home-cooked food drifted up the stairs, and Ryker's stomach rumbled. At the bottom of the steps he glanced around, hoping to see Shelby. His gut leapt. There she stood in the kitchen area, stirring something in a crockpot. No doubt her famous chili. Chili she'd won award after award with. Chili he'd eaten many times as the two of them sat on the couch near the fireplace watching a movie.

"I'm starving. Let's go eat before it's all gone."

Tyler rubbed his flat belly. At fifty-five, Tyler looked as slim and trim as any twenty-year old. Even his face was almost wrinkle-free. He needed to find out Tyler and Arlana's secret on how to stay so young looking.

"You're always hungry." Arlana playfully tapped his arm. She looked up at Ryker. "I don't know how he does it. He eats like a horse and never gains an ounce. I eat like a bird and the weight still comes on me."

"Honey, you look as good if not better than the day I married you."

"Oh, you just have to say that because you're my husband."

"No, I'm saying it because it's true."

The two of them gazed at each other with so much love in their eyes that jealousy twisted Ryker's heart. That could have been him and Shelby if things had been different.

Tyler nudged Ryker toward the growing line. As they waited their turn, they talked about the shop and Tyler made a few suggestions. When they reached the counter and tables where the food was, Ryker looked at the choices even though he knew there was only one choice for him and that was Shelby's chili. His mouth watered just thinking about it. He filled his bowl and topped it with grated cheese. Knowing Shelby always made cornbread when she served chili, he added a square of it onto a small paper plate and then speared a pickle and set it on the plate too.

Plates filled, he and the Williams went in search of a place to sit. Silently Ryker prayed that Shelby would join them. It was a long shot prayer, but God had a way of doing the impossible.

"Shelby, over here." Arlana waved her hand, motioning for Shelby to join them.

Ryker's heart jumped to his throat, praying she would.

* * *

Shelby so wanted to act as if she hadn't heard Arlana, but she refused to be rude. Plastering on a smile, she headed that direction, wondering what Arlana was up to. After all, the woman knew Ryker and Shelby's history.

She went to sit at the empty chair next to Arlana, but Arlana jumped up and sat on the other side of Tyler, leaving Shelby to sit next to Ryker.

Ryker stood, only glancing at her as he held out the chair for her. She looked into the handsome face she'd seen a million times in her dreams, and against her will and even her wishes, her heart responded with a yearning so strong it slurped the breath right out of her. Quick as a flash, she yanked her eyes from his, set her plate and drink down on the table, and numbly allowed Ryker to push the chair in for her.

Memories of dinners they'd shared, ones where he'd held out the chair for her, where they gazed into each other's eyes from across the table while holding hands and whispering their I love yous, rushed through her mind.

They were memories she tried to forget, but with little to no success.

Memories she secretly still cherished even though she knew she shouldn't because they only brought pain and heartache.

She gazed up at him standing behind her. "Thank you."

He smiled that same heart-stopping, sexy, gorgeous smile that always caused a fluttering of hummingbird wings to take flight in her stomach. And to make matters worse, her lips had the nerve to smile back at him. What was she doing? The man had broken her heart, and she needed to remember that. A blink, and her sanity returned. She turned her face away from his questioning gaze.

Ryker sat down. His broad shoulders took up a lot of room, leaving only a few inches between them. Sparks jumped from his body onto hers, igniting those old feelings she got every time she thought of him or was near him.

Every time she caught sight of him walking toward her with that swagger of confidence and that buff muscular body.

Every time he touched her.

And every time he held her in his arms, kissing her until shivers shimmied through her heart her soul and her body.

Shelby fumbled with the napkin wrapped around her silverware. She hated what was happening to her. Hated that even though he'd run out on her that she longed for things to be the way they used to be between them. If, for some bizarre reason things were the same, she would reach for his hand and hold it dearly.

She would cup his face and kiss him soundly on those soft, yet firm lips of his.

And she would tell him how much she loved him.

But all of that was just a fantasy. A thing of the past.

There would be no more kisses.

No more hand holding.

No more anything else.

For as much as she wanted it to be so, it couldn't.

She could never allow herself to be with him again. It hurt far too much, and she couldn't go through that kind of pain again. No, for the time being, she would smile and be polite even, but when this was over, she hoped she never had to see him again.

Chapter Five

Arms crossed and ankle draped across the other, Ryker leaned against Shelby's silver Nissan Terra SUV and waited for her to come out of the church. He had to talk to her. Being around her again, hearing her laughter, and having her near him without being with her was pure torment. He had to get her to listen to him, to see if they could at least try to renew the relationship they once had. If it were possible, he loved her even more than before, and he'd never even for a moment stopped loving her. And judging by the look in her eyes when she'd gazed up at him, she still felt something for him too. He recognized that look, he'd seen it often enough.

The second he spotted her stepping outside the door, carrying that bulky box, he pushed himself off her SUV and strode toward her. "Here, let me get that for you." He reached out to take it from her, but she pulled it off to the side.

"Thanks, but I've got it." She brushed past him and strode toward her Nissan.

Not one to be deterred easily, he rushed to the passenger side door, and when he heard the click of her keypad, he opened the door.

Her eyes said she didn't want him there, but her mouth never spoke the words. That alone gave him the courage he needed to press on. Without her consent, he took the box from her and set it on the seat, then closed the door.

Shelby hustled toward the driver's side.

If he didn't hurry, she'd be inside and gone before he had a chance to say anything to her. "Shelby, please don't go yet."

With her hand on the door handle, she stiffened, but didn't turn.

"Please, just let me explain why I left like I did. Then if you want me to leave you alone after that, I will. I promise." That would be the hardest promise he'd ever have to keep, but he would if that was what she wanted.

Shelby slowly turned around. Fire blazed from her eyes as she crossed her arms. "There is nothing you could possibly say that would excuse what you did to me. You hurt me, Ryker. Bad. You broke my heart and destroyed any faith and trust I had in you when you left." She shook her head. "You didn't even have the decency to tell me in person. You took the coward's way out by calling."

Ouch, that stung. But she was right. He had taken the coward's way out. With good reason. He knew if he saw the hurt in her eyes when he told her they were through, he wouldn't have had the courage to go through it, and at the time, he had to.

* * *

Emotions raged inside Shelby like a mountain thunderstorm. She couldn't stay here and listen to his excuse.

No matter what it was.

Regardless of the pleading in his blue eyes.

And yet, a part of her yearned to know. Had to know.

But not now.

Not today.

Maybe not ever.

She whirled and flung her vehicle door open. With one foot inside her car, she stopped when she heard Ryker say, "I left because I was dying."

Dying?

Ryker was dying?

Fear and horror wrapped around her heart.

With her leg cocked at a weird angle, she flopped her body onto the seat.

Ryker squatted down between the door and her. He reached for her hands and held them in his. She wanted to yank them away, but she couldn't. Feeling their warmth and strength let her know that he wasn't a ghost and that he was very much alive. She wanted to draw them to her lips and kiss them, to hold them against her cheeks.

"Shelby, I'm really sorry. I wanted to tell you in person. But you were right. I did take the coward's way out. I knew I couldn't bear to see your face when I told you."

The back of her eyes stung, but she refused to cry. She had shed enough tears over this man. Besides, she was afraid once she did, she may not stop.

Shelby locked gazes with him as determination

barreled through her. "Why didn't you tell me? How long...?" She swallowed hard, fighting back the tears that had become even more aggressive. "How long do you have?"

"However long God gives me."

"I mean," her gaze fell to her lap. "How long do the doctors give you?" Shivers overtook her body, both from the cold and from what she heard.

"Listen, you're freezing. Why don't we go someplace warm where we can talk about this in private? We can either go to your place or mine, and I'll tell you everything."

Numb as a fence post inside and out, she nodded. "Okay. I'll see you at my place." Without looking at him, she asked, "You remember how to get there, don't you?"

"I do, but I'll follow you."

Again she nodded. Twisting in her seat, she put her other leg inside, closed the door, and turned the key.

As she drove toward her house, she allowed the tears to flow. Ryker was dying. She was going to lose him again. "God, why? Why did you allow him back in my life if you knew he was dying? And just when I was starting to move on." Shelby clutched her stomach as the pain of loss tore into her.

She didn't want Ryker to know she'd been crying, that he still had the power over her to hurt her. If she continued, her red eyes and blotchy face would give it away, so using all the willpower she had, she stopped crying. She wiped her eyes and blew her nose. Turning the rear view mirror toward her, she glanced at her face.

It was red, something she could blame on the cold, but her eyes, that was a whole other story. Before she returned the mirror back into place, she checked to see if Ryker was behind her. He was, and she wasn't sure how she felt about that.

In a way she hoped he would change his mind and not come, and in another way she wanted him to, so maybe, finally she could put the pieces together that had never made sense. Ack! The whole thing was like riding the largest roller coaster in the world. Up high one minute, down low the next. Loving him one minute, despising him the next. Only this ride wasn't a joy ride, it was her life. And his.

Shelby pulled up to her log house. Even though it had started to snow on the way home, she didn't bother to park her Nissan in the garage. As soon as she shut the engine off, she hurried around to the passenger side to get the food box.

Ryker pulled up right behind her in his candy-apple red and black Hummer h2. He always did like mean looking machines and trucks. This one was definitely that with its wide aggressive tires that reminded her of the tires on a monster truck.

"Let me get that."

Shelby was too emotionally drained to argue with him, so she let him.

As they walked to her front door, past the pine trees loaded with blinking Christmas lights, Ryker strode up beside her. "Remember when we used to decorate those trees with those great big hideous ornaments, and how when we finished your dad would rearrange everything?"

"I remember. And I also remember why. It's because you were always in such a hurry that you all but threw the lights on instead of spacing them evenly like Dad wanted them."

"I know. But I had my reasons." He waggled his eyebrows. "Your dad wouldn't let you go out with me until you had your part of the decorations up. As many lights and stuff as he wanted, it would have taken all day to get finished." He glanced around. "I see you have most of the lights and decorations up already."

She looked around the yard to the life-size nativity set, the giant inflated Tigger, and snow-globe that had snowmen inside riding on the merry go round horses, the large, lighted ginger-bread house and the skimpy animated decorations. Dad usually had the yard covered with animated, moving Christmas decorations, and inflated seasonal items. "I didn't put them all up. It takes too long. I wish they were though, especially since Mom and Dad are coming up this week, and it would be so nice to have it the way Dad used to have it."

"I can help with that," he said as they reached the front door.

Shelby turned puzzled eyes up at him. She wasn't sure she wanted his help. Before she committed to something like that, she wanted to hear what he had to say first. Then, the most she could promise was she'd see how things went.

* * *

Ryker stood under the small porch. While Shelby searched for her key, he perused the place. Nothing had changed much. The big boulders that he and his dad and Shelby's dad had hauled down from the mountain with a front-end loader still lined the rustic yard. Four of the six pine trees they planted in the front yard still stood. The fresh pine scent mingling with the aroma of freshly falling snow filled his nostrils. His gaze went out to the lake. "Is the lake frozen over yet?"

"I haven't checked. But it's probably partially frozen over like it usually is this time of year."

Many evenings when the lake was frozen enough to be out there on safely, he and Shelby had ridden their sleds across the frozen water so they could get a full view of all the Christmas lights the town put up. They'd end up back here at her parents' house, where they would sit around the fire and sip peppermint mocha lattes.

Yes, this place had always evoked such wonderful memories. So many that it felt strange being back here after so long, but it also felt right at the same time. Ryker and his parents had spent a lot of time there during his time of growing up. Their parents had been best friends as far back as he could remember.

"You coming in, or are you just going to stand there and let all the heat out?"

He turned to find Shelby standing inside holding the door open. Ryker hurried inside and stepped out of the way for her to shut the door.

Max, her dog, sat next to her and eyed Ryker warily. "Hey, Max, you remember me, don't you, boy?"

Ryker set the box down on the bench inside the door. Squatting down, he slid his hand toward Max and allowed the dog to sniff him. Max's tail wagged slowly, but cautiously. Ryker wouldn't push it. He stood and looked over at Shelby. "Guess he doesn't remember me."

Her eyes narrowed. "It has been a while." With those words she turned her back to him and removed her coat and hat and hung them on the hooks. She stooped over and removed her snow boots and slipped her wool stocking-clad feet into a pair of fur-lined leather house slippers. Something she'd done for as long as he'd known her.

Without a word to him, she yanked up the box and headed toward the kitchen, her feet slapping against the knotty pine floor.

He removed his outer garments and boots and padded across the floor in his stocking feet. Something about it felt oddly familiar and yet foreign to him. Same with being inside the place. Things looked different.

The knotty pine walls and stair railings were the same, but the powder-blue leather furniture wasn't. "I don't remember all the moose and bear and wildlife stuff. Or that leather furniture." He yanked his head that direction. "When did your folks redecorate the place?"

Shelby turned from grabbing two mugs out of the cupboard and looked at him. "They didn't. I did." She grabbed the copper tea kettle off the stove, filled it with tap water, and set it on the burner. When she finished turning the burner on, she faced him. "I own this place now."

"Wow, that's a shocker. I didn't think your folks would ever sell this place. They loved it."

"They still do. They just couldn't live here anymore because Dad can't handle the altitude, so they moved down to Denver. When they said they were going to put the place on the market, I bought it." She shrugged.

A lot had sure changed in eighteen months. "Why isn't your dad able to handle the altitude anymore?" Ryker plucked a chunk of Christmas peppermint bark candy from the candy dish in front of him, popped it in his mouth and waited for her answer.

"He developed asthma, and his blood pressure went sky high too. The doctor told him he needed to move away from here and go to a lower altitude. Doc C. wanted him to move someplace near sea level, but Dad refused. He said he loved his mountains too much. Denver was as far as he would go."

"That sounds like your dad. Stubborn as ever." They both laughed. Hearing Shelby's laughter brought joy to his heart. "You said he was coming up here this week. Is he doing better?"

"He's doing much better. He lost a bunch of weight and that helped. He still can't handle being up here for very long though because of the asthma."

"I'm glad to hear he's doing better, but it's too bad about the asthma."

Ryker didn't know what else to say and apparently Shelby didn't either. He popped another piece of peppermint bark into his mouth and focused on the taste and feel of the crunchy yet creamy smooth texture.

"I see you still love that stuff. I never could stand it

because of the dark chocolate."

"Why do you have it around then?"

Shelby's cheeks flushed, and her eyelids lowered. The tea kettle whistled, she whirled and scurried toward the stove as if a fire were licking her heels.

Had she kept that candy around because it reminded her of him? As far as he knew, no one else in her family cared for it. Hope sparked through him at the thought.

"I'm sorry I don't have the stuff to make peppermint lattes, so this will have to do." Holding a box of hot chocolate in each hand, she turned to him. "You want peppermint hot chocolate or regular?"

"What do you think?"

She dumped a package of the peppermint flavor into a bear mug. Holding the tea kettle over the cup, she poured the steaming hot water into it. "Just making sure." She shifted her attention onto him and her hand followed.

Water ran over the side of the mug and onto the floor.

"Shelby, watch out!" His adrenaline kicked into gear. He darted around the island bar but was too late.

Hot water landed on top of her foot.

Shelby screamed.

Ryker took the kettle from her hand and set it on the stove. Dropping to his knee, he removed her moccasin and damp sock as fast and as carefully as he could, then scooped her into his arms. The skin by her ankle wasn't broken so he hurried to the sink, made sure the temperature of the water was cool, and stuck her foot under the running water.

Heart pounding in his ears, his eyes went to hers. Shelby's glance went down, then up, then to his mouth, then back to his eyes. Longing filled those brown eyes of hers.

He could relate.

Love for this woman surged through him, and the urge to kiss her bulldozed over him. An urge he had to stifle.

His focus gyrated to her foot which had now turned a bright red. "We need to get you to the doctor."

"No." She stopped him and looked down at her foot. "I've had worse burns than this. Besides, they'll just put some burn cream on and wrap it up. I can do that myself." She raised her foot, but before she it got completely out of the stream of water, Ryker stopped her.

"You need to leave it under that water at least ten or fifteen minutes. While you do that, I'll go get the cream."

"It's in the medicine closet. You remember where that is, don't you?"

"I do."

She nodded.

Although he didn't want to let her go, he settled her on the cabinet and headed to the medicine closet. His words 'I do' followed him. With any luck someday he would speak those two words to her and forever join their lives together.

* * *

Shelby's foot throbbed. She fought back the tears. Tears not caused by the pain in her foot, but by the yearning of her heart. Having Ryker hold her in his strong arms brought back a longing so deep she could barely stand it. She hated that she still loved him, still wanted him.

That he still had control of her heart.

She wished she totally and completely despised him, it would make things so much easier. But she didn't. She loved him as much, if not more than she ever did, but the fear of trusting him again and giving him power over her heart again scared her to death.

Ryker returned carrying the burn cream, gauze, tape, and a bottle of ibuprofen. Seeing him in her house in his stocking feet bothered her. It was too intimate. Too familiar. She needed to get him out of here. Out of her life for good. But could she really find it in herself to do it?

It was all so confusing and intoxicating too.

While Ryker tended to her foot, the familiar aroma of his pinewood cologne floated up her nostrils and swirled through her senses. And seeing the shape of his bulging muscle under his flannel shirt when he flexed his arm had her wanting to feel it like she used to. She loved those large muscled arms and muscular legs. Ryker worked out hard to get the body he had. In fact, they used to work out together.

"There. All done." He screwed the lid back on the burn cream jar and set it with the rest of the items. He filled a glass with water and handed her two ibuprofen. Their fingers brushed when she took the glass from him.

Inwardly she sighed at the effect that one small gesture caused in her. She avoided his eyes so he wouldn't see just how much it had affected her and downed the pills.

Shelby gasped when he suddenly scooped her into his arms. Her arm flew around his neck to help balance herself. "What are you doing?"

"Taking you to the living room."

"I can walk."

"And I can carry you."

How could she argue with that logic?

Max's toenails clicked across the floor as he walked beside them.

Ryker sat her down in one of the recliners near the fireplace and turned to go.

"What are you doing?"

"That's twice you've asked me that now." He smiled. "I'm going to get our hot chocolate."

"Oh." She nodded.

It almost seemed natural to see Ryker in her kitchen fixing the two of them hot chocolate. He'd done it a million times before. Only back then it was lattes. Well, this wasn't back then, this was now. Still, for now, she would enjoy every moment with him because all this ended today. It had to. She had to guard her heart even more because he was dying.

He handed her a cup, set his down on a wildlife coaster, and strolled to the moss rock fireplace. Shelby wasn't going to ask a third time what he was doing. She knew. It was one of those things they'd done a bazillion times before.

She watched as he laid the logs and newspaper methodically and strategically before taking the long stemmed fireplace match to it. Within minutes the fire blazed, cracked and popped and sent sparks up the chimney as the pinesap burned. Shelby curled her legs off to the side, placing her injured foot on top of the other.

Ryker lowered his tall frame onto the chair across from her. Neither said a word, they stared at the fire and sipped their beverages.

Unable to bear not knowing any longer, Shelby gathered up the courage she needed to ask the question she dreaded, yet needed to know the answer to. "So how long do you have?"

Ryker looked over at her, contentment shrouded him. "How long do I have for what?"

"To live."

"Oh, that." Ryker set his cup down, leaned his elbows on his knees, and clasped his hands together. "I was never terminally ill."

"What?" Shelby shot up and off the chair and immediately regretted her hasty movement as pain shot through her foot. But it would have to wait. She slammed her hands on her hips. "Get out!"

His brows darted upward. "What?"

"You heard me. I said, get out." She pointed toward the front door.

"Shelby, I'm not leaving here until you hear what I have to say about what happened."

"I don't want to know. You lied to me. Now get out!"

"Lied to you? About what?"

"Earlier you said you were dying and that's why you left me. And now you just said you weren't terminally ill." Angry tears flooded her eyes and she didn't bother to stop them.

"Shelby, please don't cry." He took a step toward her.

Shelby jumped back out of the way. "Don't touch me." She strode toward the front door, ignoring the pain slicing through her foot. She wanted him out of her life and she wanted him out now. Why she ever allowed him back in even for those few brief moments was beyond her. Well, it would never happen again.

She yanked his coat off of the rack and held it toward him.

"Shelby, I said I'm not leaving until you listen to what I have to say." Coming all the way to her, he pushed the coat down to her side, gazing at her with a firmness that curled her toes. "Then if you still want me to go, I will, but not until then."

"Fine." She crossed her arms over her chest. "Whatever. Just hurry up and get it over with, then leave." She glared at him, waiting for him to say what he had to say so he would leave and never come back.

Ryker scrubbed his fingers across his forearm. "Shortly before I left, I went to the doctor because I found a lump. He sent me to a surgeon who removed it. I waited and waited for them to call me with the results, but after almost a week of not hearing anything, I called him and he said the results weren't in yet. I thought that was strange because when Randy found out he had cancer, his tests came back within a day or two. When the doctor finally did call he said I had a rare fast acting type of lymphoma cancer."

A pit filled Shelby's stomach. "Cancer?" She swallowed back the lump in her throat. His brother Randy had died of cancer. "Did—did you get a second opinion?"

Ryker shook his head as pain flooded through his eyes. "They had more than one lab run independent tests because that particular cancer is so rare, and each came back with the same conclusion. Most people who have that type of cancer don't live long at all, and some even die during chemo treatments."

"Why didn't you tell me?" She had to know the answer to that question. Everything rode on his answer.

"For several reasons, Shelby. One, I couldn't bear the thought of you suffering like I did with Randy. Two, watching a loved one die a slow painful death and not be able to do anything about it is the worst possible thing a person can go through. I didn't want that for you, Shelby." He rubbed at his forearm again. A sure sign he was uncomfortable. "Three, I didn't want to leave you a widow. And four, I didn't want to risk fathering a child just to then leave them fatherless. I couldn't take those risks. I just couldn't." Regret and pain furrowed his brow.

She wanted to ask a million more questions, but she couldn't bear seeing him hurting so badly. In two steps, she was in front of him, wrapping her arms around him. "Oh, Ryker, I'm so sorry."

His arms slipped around her and he pulled her to

him. He held onto her as if holding onto a lifeline. The urge to kiss away his pain whirled inside her.

No longer able to control her emotions, she gave into her desire to comfort him with her kiss. Something that always worked in the past. She leaned her head back and gazed up at him.

His eyes, full of questions and hope, snagged onto hers.

She rose on her tiptoes and settled her mouth onto his. A massive fireworks display couldn't even come close to the sparks bouncing across her heart. All the years of missing him and yearning for him flowed through her kisses, and he responded in kind. The fervency of their kiss melted her insides like a snowman baking in the hot sun.

Every part of her wanted him, but she refused to give into that temptation and sin against the Lord. Instead, breathlessly, she removed her mouth from his, but not her arms, and settled her head against his chest. His heartbeat pounded in her ear. His rapid pulse matched her own.

What was she going to do? She couldn't let him go now. But even knowing his reasons for why he left, how could she trust him not to leave her again if, God forbid, something ever came up like that again? *God, help me.*

Chapter Six

Ryker rose bright and early. He wanted to surprise Shelby by putting up the rest of the Christmas decorations today.

The night before had been emotionally draining for both of them. After he told her why he'd left, and Shelby had kissed him like she had, he knew he had to leave. He'd seen the same desire in her eyes that he himself had battled. The Bible was clear about fleeing temptation. So, he had. Since they were both exhausted, they decided they would talk more later.

He turned his pickup into the half-moon driveway covered with six inches of freshly fallen snow and parked in front. Excitement swirled through his gut like autumn leaves caught in a dust devil at the prospect of seeing Shelby again. A part of him wondered what kind of reception he'd get today.

Whistling *It's beginning to look a lot like Christmas* he strode up the walk feeling lighter and happier than he had in the last eighteen months.

He rang the doorbell and stepped back.

He could hear Max barking inside and noticed movement at the big picture window.

Max peered his head out from behind the curtain, barking.

"Somebody here, boy?" Shelby's voice sounded on

the other side of the door.

When she swung it open, her eyes widened. "Ryker, what are you doing here? And so early." Her hand flew to her disheveled hair. She gathered it all together and twisted it to where it hung in the front. She stood there blinking, wearing powder-blue plaid flannel pajamas and an open fleece robe with the belt hanging down each side.

"I guess it's a little too early for me to show up, huh?" His lips quivered with a hidden smile.

Her focus dropped to her attire. She quickly overlapped the lapels of her robe and drew the belt into a knot. "I—I'm usually up and dressed by now."

"I remember. Can I come in? It's cold out here."

"Oh I'm sorry. Where are my manners?" She moved aside and Ryker stepped inside. The aromas of bacon and fresh brewed coffee filled the room.

He made a show of sniffing the air. "It seems like I made it just in time for breakfast."

"What are you doing here?"

"You already asked me that. But I'll give you that one because I never answered you. I came to do the rest of the decorations. That way the house will be all finished the way your dad likes it when they get here."

Her eyes brightened. "That's so sweet. But you don't have to. Dad will understand."

"I know I don't have to, I want to."

She chewed on her lip. "Dad would be so surprised." Indecision tumbled across her face.

"He sure would." Ryker removed his boots. Shelby and Max followed him as he made his way to the kitchen to snag a piece of bacon like he had so many times before. Only difference this time, Mrs. Davis usually stood there with a plate all ready for him. She'd hear his voice and fix him a plate. All he had to do was sit at the table and eat it. It was the same with Shelby at his family's house.

"Help yourself. I'm going to run upstairs and change."

Ryker grabbed a piece of bacon off the plate. Holding it mid-air he asked, "Why? You look fine to me."

Shelby rolled her eyes. "Don't be ridiculous. I'm not going to stand around here in my pajamas while a gorgeous man is standing in my kitchen."

"Where?" Ryker looked around, grinning the whole time.

"You know where. You. Now, I'm going to run and get dressed." She whirled around and tossed over her shoulder the words, "I know how you love bacon, so save me a piece."

"I'm not making any promises, so you'd better hurry," he hollered to her back.

She raised her hand in the air and sashayed to her room.

Ryker took a bite and closed his eyes, savoring the crunchy morsel. When he opened his eyes, Max stared up at him with those pitiful eyes. "You want a piece, boy?" Ryker broke off a chunk and handed it to the dog.

Max took it gently from his hand.

"Don't tell, Shelby."

"Don't tell Shelby what?" Shelby came out of her

bedroom with her hair in a ponytail and wearing a white turtleneck sweater and faded blue jeans. She looked very pretty and very sexy in that outfit.

A glance down at Max and then back up to him, Shelby puckered her forehead. "You aren't feeding my dog bacon, are you?"

Ryker pressed his hand against his chest. "Me? Would I do something like that?"

Her head bobbed. "Yes. Yes, you would."

"Okay, you caught me. Guilty as charged. What's the punishment for my crime?"

Shelby stepped up to him and cupped his face. "This." She kissed him until he found himself shifting his body up against the counter to support himself. When her lips left his, he let out a long breath. Quick as a flash, he snatched up another piece of bacon and said, "Here, Max, you can have the whole piece." And he tossed it to the dog who leapt in the air and caught it. Then he turned his puckered lips to Shelby. "I'm waiting for my punishment."

Shelby shook her head and smiled. "What am I going to do with you?"

"Love me."

Shelby's smile slipped, she turned her back to him, picked up a piece of bacon, and put distance between them as she bit into it.

Ryker inwardly groaned. *Me and my big mouth.*

He knew he needed to go slow, to earn back Shelby's trust in him. She'd as much as said so the night before.

Wanting to lighten the mood and to clear the air of

the heaviness hovering around them, he cleared his throat. "Got any eggs to go with that bacon?"

Shelby turned around. The playfulness of just moments ago gone. "Yes, there's some in the pan on the stove. Help yourself."

Ryker stepped up behind her and settled his hands on her shoulders. Hers landed on top of his, and he wondered if she was aware of what she'd done. "Shelby, I'm sorry. I didn't mean to make you uncomfortable. I'm not expecting you to love me after what I did. I'm just hoping you can find it in your heart to forgive me, and to give us another chance. If you're willing to try again, we could go out to see where this thing leads. Do you think you can do that?" he asked softly.

Shelby took three steps away and turned. With her eyes downcast, she said, "I don't know, Ryker. There's a part of me that wants to, but I'm scared. Scared that you'll leave me again, and I can't go through that again. Once was bad enough."

"Listen, I would never do that to you again." Ryker went to take a step forward but she held up her hand.

"I can't promise you anything right now, Ryker."

"I'm not looking for you to promise me anything. Nor am I asking you for forever. Right now, I'm only asking for Saturday night."

"Saturday night?" She looked up at him, her brows veed. "What's Saturday night?"

"A Christmas party I'm throwing at the Lodge."

"I don't know."

"C'mon, it'll be fun. Okay, probably not fun, but would you go with me? I hate going to these benefit things alone." He sent her his best puppy dog look. Before, she could never resist it.

"Benefit? What benefit?"

"Well, since you and the search and rescue team saved my life, I wanted to return the favor by hosting a benefit fund raiser for them. The whole county's invited. I've prepared my folk's lodge, hired a caterer, and everything."

A soft smile played just under her dour expression. "How could I say no to that? After all, it is for a good cause." She tugged at her lip. "Okay, I'll go. But," she held up her hand. "No promises, okay?"

"You got it." Joy flooded through his heart. This was a start. "Shall we seal it with a kiss?"

She sent him a warning, albeit playful look. He held up his hands in surrender. "Have it your way." He winked.

* * *

That wink of his always melted Shelby's insides and caused her heart to flutter. She was nervous about committing to a date with Ryker, but how could she turn down a benefit for something she believed so strongly in? Besides, she knew she had to give them a try, or she would regret it the rest of her life. But, she would go slowly and if she saw any sign that he couldn't be trusted, that was it. It would be over for good between them this time. "Let's eat. I'm starving."

After breakfast, they bundled up and headed to the storage area above the rafters in the garage. Her father had built the ceiling to act like a floor. Shelby braced the ladder against the rafter opening and climbed the rungs. "I'll hand them down to you." She scanned the area until she spotted the rest of the Christmas decorations. Crouching over, she headed to where the boxes marked *Christmas Decorations* set. One by one she scooted them to the opening and handed them down to Ryker.

When she finished gathering everything, she started down the ladder. Halfway down, Ryker hoisted her down the rest of the way.

His large hands remained on her waist, and he gazed into her eyes. The love she'd seen in them years ago, shone in them now.

She wasn't quite sure what to do about that. His eyes went to her mouth. Excitement and trepidation flitted into her stomach. She wanted to kiss him, badly, but she also battled with where to draw the line on how much kissing they should do until she felt certain she could trust him with her heart again. After all, he'd left once with what he believed to be a good reason. What would stop him from doing it again?

Ryker took possession of her mouth and kissed her tenderly and slowly. Seconds later, he released her lips, and rested his forehead against hers. "Thanks for not pulling away."

What could she say to that?

You're welcome?

Kiss me again?

No, don't kiss me again?

Yes, please do?

Ack! The whole thing was all so discombobulating.

"Well," she said, turning around and planting her gloved hands on her hips. "We have our work cut out for us, now don't we?"

"We sure do. We'd better get busy if we're going to get it all done before dark."

They spent the majority of the day putting up the remaining decorations inside and outside until the only thing left was the Christmas tree. "Do you want to go get a tree?"

"Today?" Shelby looked up him. "Are you crazy? I'm tired."

"When are your folks coming?"

"Not until Thursday. Why?"

"You want to do it tomorrow then? We could make a day of it. I could haul our sleds in my trailer, and we could ride for a couple of hours and then cut down a tree. What do you say?" The lines of just how slowly or fast she could or should take this blurred with the vision of his sweet eyes.

"I say it sounds like fun. That'll give me Wednesday to decorate it, and then I can head over to City Market in Granby." She chuckled. "I invited the McIntyre's over for dinner Friday night. Mr. McIntyre is hoping to beat Dad at Monopoly."

Ryker laughed. "Like that's ever going to happen."

"You know it, and I know it, but you can't blame Mr. McIntyre for hoping now, can you? Hey, you want to join us?"

"I'd love to. If you need help with anything just let me know."

"You've already helped enough. Getting the

decorations up is a biggy and doing the tree is too." She clapped her hands like a child opening the wished-for gift on Christmas morning. "I can hardly wait to see Dad's face. You want to stay for supper? There's left over chili." She knew she rattled her sentences out, but she was so excited, and now she was looking forward to Christmas. Before, she'd dreaded the holiday, but Ryker's being here had a lot to do with her excitement. *Whoa, slow down there, Shelby. Remember to keep your guard up and to guard your heart just in case.*

"Now would I ever turn down an opportunity to eat your chili?"

"True, very true. Silly of me to ask, huh?" She hurried to the kitchen and pulled the container of leftover chili out of the fridge and set it on the counter. "Wait, I just thought of something. I'm not keeping you from work or anything, am I?"

"Nope. The guys are running the shop for me."

"Oh good, I'm glad." She couldn't believe how much she sounded like a silly school girl, but for the first time in eighteen months she felt like one. And for today, she was going to allow herself to enjoy that feeling.

* * *

Ryker patted his rock solid stomach. "I've eaten a lot of chili in my lifetime but none as delicious as yours. What's your secret?"

"It's not a secret really. But you promise not to tell anyone what I put in mine?"

"I promise." With his arms on the table he leaned

toward her.

"Elk meat."

"That's elk in there?"

"Yep. I cook it in the crock pot all day with the seasonings and stuff, and you can't even tell the difference between it and beef. A lot of people wouldn't eat it if they knew it had elk meat though." She shook her finger at him. "So don't you go telling anyone. You promised."

"I won't." Ryker's phone rang. He pulled it out of his pocket and glanced at the screen and frowned. "Hey, Jeff, what's up?"

"Sorry to bother you, but two of your Polaris RMK PRO 800's didn't come back."

Ryker stood and went to the window. He peered out into the pitch dark night. "What time were they supposed to be back?"

"At four-thirty. It's after five now. I tried calling their cells, but no one answers. I hate to say this, Ryker, but I think they stole them."

"What makes you say that?" Ryker paced back and forth in front of the big picture window, raking his fingers across his forearm.

"Well, their truck was parked out in front earlier and now it isn't."

"They could have had someone meet them or something."

"I thought the same thing, until..." Jeff let the sentence hang.

"Until what?"

"Until I ran their driver's license and plate numbers.

They're registered to different people."

Ryker groaned. Two of his best machines. Ones he'd purchased, hoping to get the more experienced rider's business. He should have listened to Tyler. Tyler warned him not to rent such expensive machines out. "Call the sheriff. I'll be there as soon as I can."

"Sorry, Ryker."

"Don't be. It's not your fault. I'll talk to you in a few." He hung up.

"What's wrong?" Shelby asked, lines creased her forehead.

"I think someone just stole two of my newest and best sleds."

"Oh no. Which ones?"

"My Polaris RMK PRO 800's."

"Ouch."

"Ouch is right."

"Is there anything I can do?"

"No. I've got to get over to the shop." Ryker strode toward the front door. He quickly put on his boots and coat. He hated for the evening to end especially like this, but he didn't have any choice. "I'll see you tomorrow." He kissed her cheek and headed outside. Inches of the heavy snowfall covered the road. Surely with this much accumulation, the men who stole his sleds couldn't have gotten too far.

Lights were on inside the shop when he pulled up in front. Only Jeff's truck was out front. The sheriff hadn't gotten there yet. Ryker hurried inside, and the bell tinkled when he opened the door.

Jeff met him as he walked in. His face had aged ten

years since he last saw him. "The sheriff will be here as soon as he can. He's on another call right now. Man, I'm really sorry, Ryker. The picture on his license matched his face. I had no way of knowing it was a fake ID."

Ryker laid his hand on Jeff's shoulder and squeezed it. "It's not your fault. You did what you were supposed to and that was to get their driver's license number and plate." He hooked his hand over his chin. "I've got to figure out a system where we can run them before we rent out the sleds. What kind of vehicle did they have?"

"A half-ton Chevy pickup. Super cab. White."

"Well that narrows it down." Oh man, this was going to be even more difficult that he originally thought. "There has to be hundreds of them around. Anything unique about it that you might have noticed?"

"Well, it had a lift kit on it and sat up pretty high." Jeff stroked his goatee. "Chrome spokes rims with wide tires. I'm guessing 35x14.00x15 Super Swampers. They looked a lot like the ones I have on my truck. But that's about all I can remember."

"That's pretty good. Every little bit will help. Good job, Jeff."

The shop phone rang. Jeff snatched it up.

"Yeah, he's here. Just a minute." Jeff handed the phone to Ryker.

"This is Ryker."

"Ryker, I'm glad I caught you." Shelby sounded relieved. "I talked to Tim and told him and his friends to keep a look out for your machines. He said he saw a couple of Polaris RMK PRO 800's earlier heading down the mountain over Berthoud Pass. The only reason he noticed them was because the guys were driving recklessly and sliding all over the place. In fact, they almost ran him off the road when they passed him."

"Did he happen to say what kind of vehicle they drove?"

"Yes, a white Chevy pickup. He said it sat up pretty high. That was about all he could see."

"Thanks, Shelby. I owe you one."

"You don't owe me anything. I just want to see you get your machines back."

"I'll call the state patrol. Talk to you later. Love you."

Ryker hung up, and his gut twisted. He just told Shelby he loved her again. He only hoped those words didn't scare her away for good.

Not having time to dwell on it, he called the state patrol and pretty much got the run around, with them saying how busy they were with the weather and all, but they did finally say they would see what they could do, and they'd put out a bulletin on the vehicle. Well, he wasn't going to wait for them. "I'm going down the mountain and look for those thieving snakes."

"Want me to go with you?" Jeff asked.

"No, I'd rather you stay here and take care of things."

"Be careful, man. If you find them, things could get ugly."

"I will." With those words Ryker left, prepared to do battle if necessary.

* * *

All last evening, and even through her restless sleep, Ryker's words 'love you' played over and over in Shelby's brain. They were words she wanted to hear, wanted to trust in, but didn't fully yet. She'd trusted in them before, and at the first sign of something major, he was gone. Like now.

The night before, she tried to call Ryker's phone but he didn't answer. They were supposed to spend the day together looking for a tree and going for a ride.

The clock chimed nine times. Here it was 9:00 am and he was supposed to be here way before now. Where was he? She didn't want to be a pest and keep calling him. After all, she'd already left several messages. This felt like déjà vu all over again. Only the last time, a recorded message said he had left and wouldn't be back. This time, Ryker hadn't even left a message, but the fear was there just the same as if he had.

Was she overreacting? Being ridiculous? Was Ryker tied up with the missing snowmobile incident?

If so, why hadn't he called her to let her know?

And why wasn't he answering her calls? Was it her, the calls, or something else that kept him from answering?

Was he okay?

Shelby tugged at her lip until it ached.

Not knowing what was going on was driving her batty.

Well, she couldn't wait around all day for him to call. If he didn't call her soon, she would head out and go get a tree by herself, or she'd just buy one off the lot.

She'd give him one hour. No more. And then, with or without him, she was going.

Max followed her as she flew through her house, cleaning and wiping everything and anything she could think of just to keep busy and to keep her mind off of where Ryker was.

Her phone rang. Shelby darted over to it and snatched up the receiver. "Hello."

"Hi, sweetheart."

"Mom." Disappointment flushed through her that it wasn't Ryker like she had hoped it was.

"Are you okay? You sound upset?"

"I'm okay. I just thought this was Ry—" She stopped herself from saying his name, realizing she hadn't even told her mom about Ryker being back in her life.

"This was who, Shelby?"

She wasn't sure how she would tell her mom about him. Her parents had hoped and prayed that the two of them would get back together. Shelby didn't want to get their hopes up as she herself didn't know if they would or not.

Why did life have to be so complicated?

"Shelby, you there?"

She blinked and gave herself a mental shake. "Yes, I'm here."

"I just wanted to let you know that Dad and I are coming up today instead of tomorrow. If that's okay with you."

"Of course it is. I can't wait to see you and Daddy."

"How are the roads?"

"It snowed quite a bit last night. We got about nine inches of fresh powder. But, you've driven in a lot worse."

"Well, we don't let something like a little snow stop us from seeing our daughter."

"I'm glad. But be careful, okay?"

"Okay, we'll probably leave here about eleven thirty or so."

"Great. See you soon. Love you, Mom."

"Love you too, sweetie."

Shelby hung up her phone. If she hurried, she'd have enough time to get to City Market. She'd grab a tree there. City Market usually had some pretty nice ones for sale. She would have liked to have cut one down, but she didn't have enough time, and she refused to wait around even one more minute for Ryker.

Her jaw clenched.

Couldn't the man at least have the decency to call her back? After all, they did have plans.

Well, as far as she was concerned, Ryker could just go and kiss a duck. Shelby's mother always said that whenever she was upset or mad. Right now, Shelby was both.

Chapter Seven

Ryker continued to search through the deep snow for his phone. The night before, when his vehicle had gone off the road and he had gotten stuck, he had dug for quite some time to try to get it out. When he decided he needed a tow truck, he reached for his phone in his pocket, but it wasn't there. Using his flashlight, he tried to find it, but no luck. He'd made sure the exhaust was clear and figured he would try again in the morning.

The sun barely peeked over the mountain. Bitter cold filled his lungs when he stepped outside the warm cab to search for his phone. Hard telling where it went the way he had slung the snow around with his shovel. He should have never gone after those snowmobile thieves, and should have let the state patrol, as annoying as they were, handle it. Now because of his stupidity, he'd ended up spending the night in his pickup, in a blizzard, on some backwoods road in the middle of nowhere. Thank God he had two full gas tanks when he'd set out or things could have turned ugly.

By now, Shelby was probably worried sick about him.

Once again he'd failed her.

Several minutes later, he spotted a speck of black sticking out of the snow near the base of the tree where he'd slung the majority of snow. Using his gloved hands, he dug around the black spot and retrieved his phone. Again he was thankful he'd purchased one those non-destructible types. This thing had been in the snow all night and it still worked. Now, he hoped got reception out here. Where-ever here was.

First he got his coordinates, next he called for a tow truck, and then he rang Shelby's house. Four rings and the answering machine picked it up.

"Oh, man." He left a message for her to call him. Why hadn't he thought to ask for her cell phone number? The old one no longer worked. He rubbed his chin. Who could he call to get ahold of her for him? Off the top of his head, he couldn't think of anyone. Unless... He quickly called his shop. "Jeff, good I'm glad I got you. Could you do me a favor?"

"Man, where you at? I've been trying to call you for hours."

Ryker filled him in on what all had happened and how he had his cell turned off to save the battery.

"Do you need me to come get you?"

"No, I've already called for a tow truck. I was wondering if you could run over to Shelby's to see if she's home. I tried the house and she doesn't answer, but maybe she's outside. Would you mind doing that for me? Mike can watch the shop while you're gone."

"Sure, no problem. Did you try her cell?"

"I don't have the number."

"I can call Hailey and see if she has it?"

"You have Hailey's number?"

"Yeah, I've had it for a while."

Ryker didn't even ask why. He'd seen the way they

looked at each other. "Could you give her a quick call and call me back."

"Sure will." He disconnected the call.

Ryker looked at his pickup still embedded in the snow at a weird angle. There was no way he could have dug himself out of this one. His gaze went up the long winding road buried in at least a foot of snow. Pine and Aspen trees surrounded it. Those men were up that road somewhere.

He dialed the state patrol and told them about it. They said they'd meet him up there in an hour or so and to not do anything. Like he could, he thought as he agreed before ending the call.

Ryker's cell rang. It was Jeff. "Hey, did you get it?"

"Sure did, but you owe me?"

"What do you mean I owe you?"

"Hailey said it would cost me. Dinner and a movie."

Ryker laughed. "I'm sure I can swing that."

"Nah, you don't have to. I'm just kidding."

"Hey, it'll be worth every penny and more to be able to get in touch with Shelby. I'll gladly pay it." As Jeff read the number, Ryker punched it into his phone. "Thanks, man."

"Welcome. Sure you don't need any help?"

"No, the tow truck should be here in about an hour and he's got a plow on the front. The state patrol's coming too. So, no, I'll be fine. Thanks anyway."

"Okay, well good luck catching those guys."

"Thanks. Talk to you later."

Ryker rang Shelby's cell.

"Hi, this is Shelby. Can't take your call right now,

but after the beep leave your name, number, and a short message and I'll get back to you. Thanks. Bye."

"Oh, man," Ryker groaned.

Beeeep.

"Shelby, this is Ryker. I'm sorry it took so long to call you, but I just found my phone. It's a long story, and I don't have time to tell it now. My phone battery's low, and I forgot my car charger. I'll tell you all about it when I see you later. Sorry about today. I don't know what time I'll be over. It'll probably be late this afternoon or early evening. I'll call you when I get into town. Love you. Bye."

* * *

Shelby's phone rang, but she was driving so she refused to answer it. She'd check to see who called when she arrived at City Market. At the far end of town, she turned off of Highway 40 into the snow-packed parking lot at City Market and parked her truck.

Piles of snow lined the parking lot area, and there was already a new dusting outlining the tire marks of the other vehicles.

The plows had obviously tried to clear most of the fresh snow off the parking lot but a layer of hard-packed snow remained underneath. With the freezing cold temps, it wouldn't be melting anytime soon either.

Shelby called her parents to tell them to be careful because the roads were really bad. Although they were used to driving them, she didn't want them taking any chances. In fact, she'd even tried to talk them into waiting until tomorrow to come up, but they wouldn't hear of it. "Lord, send your angels to go before them, to be their rear guard. Clear the roads of any unforeseen danger. Please, place a hedge of protection around and about them and give them driving privileges to get up here safely. And wherever Ryker is, please be with him." Worry snaked around her heart as she wondered if Ryker was okay.

Maybe it was him who'd tried to call when she was driving. She quickly checked to see if it was. Not recognizing the number, she decided that message could wait. She had lots to do.

After picking out a tree, she hurried through the store and gathered all the supplies and food she needed for Friday's dinner party and for her folk's visit. She could hardly wait. She hadn't seen her parents since May.

Driving carefully, she made her way back home. When she pulled in the drive, she expected to see Ryker's truck, but it wasn't there. By now, her anger had turned to fear. Fear that something might have happened to him.

As fast as she could, she unloaded the groceries and grabbed the Grand County phone book. She hurried to the page where she'd circled in red the snowmobile shop's number she'd found the day before.

One ring.

Two rings.

"C'mon, pick up the phone." She tugged at her lower lip.

The minute she heard a man's voice on the other

end, she blurted. "Is Ryker there?"

"Shelby? Is that you?"

"Yes. Who's this?"

"Jeff."

"Jeff, oh, I didn't even recognize your voice." It was the same voice that had answered the shop phone yesterday. "What are you doing there?"

"I work here."

"Since when?"

"Since a few days ago."

"Oh, okay. Hey, listen, is Ryker there?"

"No. Didn't he call you?"

"No. Oh wait. I got a phone call from a number I didn't recognize." She put her phone on speaker and found that number and read it to Jeff.

"That's Ryker's cell."

Oh no. She wished she would have listened to the message. Stupid telemarketers. They'd taught her not to call back numbers she didn't recognize. "Have you talked to him this morning? Is he all right?

"Yeah, he's fine. He went after those guys who stole his machines and got stuck."

"He did what?" How could he have done something so stupid?

"Yeah, can't blame him. I would have too."

Must be a guy thing, she rolled her eyes.

"Still can't believe he caught up to them. They had a pretty good head start," Jeff added.

How had Ryker accomplished that? She'd find that out later. She was just relieved to hear that Ryker was okay.

"He's waiting for a tow truck and for the state patrol to show up. Listen, a customer just walked in, I have to let you go."

"Okay. Thanks, Jeff. I'll talk to you later." She ended the call and then listened to Ryker's message. She wanted to call him back, to hear his voice, to make sure he really was okay, but he said his battery was low, so she didn't. Instead, she got busy putting groceries away. The whole time she berated herself for letting him back into her life.

Would she ever be able to trust him again?

If they got back together again, every time she didn't hear from him, would she worry and be afraid that he'd left her again? And could she really handle living like that? Was love worth the heartache and pain? She wasn't sure.

Shelby groaned.

Why did love have to be so complicated?

Why couldn't she just trust Ryker again and tell him how much she loved him and how much she wanted to be with him? Wanted to marry him? But that wasn't likely to happen any time soon.

Tired of going around that mountain for the fiftieth time since Ryker's return, Shelby glanced around the house, looking for something to keep her mind off of him.

The wood floors sparkled.

Not a speck of dust anywhere.

Throw rugs were vacuumed clean.

Everything looked great for when her folks arrived.

She had even put a pot roast in the oven.

Only one thing left to do, the tree.

So much for getting her mind off of Ryker. They were going to get a tree today and put it up together. Should she wait for him so that they could do it together?

She glanced at the clock. Two-thirty-three. She wondered where he was and how things were going. Too bad she couldn't call him, but she didn't dare waste his battery. Besides, he said he would call when he got into town.

Since her folks had called earlier to say they probably wouldn't be there until about six, she decided to go ahead and put up the tree and decorate it by herself.

An hour and half later, Shelby stood back to admire her work. Hundreds of colored lights winked back at her. Silver garland snaked around the tree. Powder-blue glass bulbs and wildlife creatures filled every almost nook and cranny of the full blue spruce. "Dad will sure be surprised," she whispered. "And so will Ryker." Max dug his nose into the palm of her hand. Shelby glanced down at her dog. "Sure looks good, doesn't it, boy?" Max licked her hand and she chuckled.

"Now." She clasped her hands together and pulled them to her chest. "Time to clean up this mess before everyone gets here." Shelby hurried to pick up the boxes, running them out to the garage and stacking them in the corner. No way would she climb that ladder without anyone around. She'd already fallen off it once this year already.

With two hours to go before her folks arrived, Shelby pulled out her recipe book and made a double batch of fudge to go along with the sugar cookies she'd baked a couple of weeks ago and had frozen. Once the fudge was made, she decorated the sugar cookies.

Max barked, Shelby jerked at the sound. He ran to the window, and using his nose, he shoved the curtain off to the side to peer outside.

"It's okay, boy. It's probably Mom and Dad."

She put the last dish away when the doorbell rang. Drying her hands on the dish towel, she hung it up and headed to the door and opened it. There stood her mom, dad, and Ryker with their arms loaded with boxes and bags.

"Look who we found standing out here." Mom yanked her head toward Ryker.

Shelby blinked. "How? What? Huh?" She frowned, not understanding what was going on and why Ryker was with her parents.

"Well, if you'll let us in, we'll tell you how, what, and huh." Mom laughed.

Shelby shook herself out of her stupor and opened the door fully. "What are you doing ringing the doorbell anyway?" She stepped out of their way and reached for some of the bags her mother had.

"This is your home now." Mom kissed her on the cheek, and then whispered in her ear. "Be nice."

Shelby knew what Mom meant by 'be nice'. Mom didn't know she'd already seen Ryker before this evening. Her gaze went to Ryker. Dark circles under his eyes indicated he hadn't slept much, and tired blanketed his every move.

"Where do you want these things?" her dad asked from behind her.

Shelby peered over Ryker's shoulder and looked at her dad. "What is that?"

"Presents. Food. Everything including the kitchen sink. You know your mother."

Shelby's glance went to her mom. "Mom, I told you not to bring anything, that I had everything under control."

"I know you did. I didn't bring much."

Shelby looked at all the presents and hiked her brow at her mother.

"I mean, I didn't bring a lot of food this time. Only a ham, a turkey, some potatoes and some baked goodies. That's all."

"That's all? That's too much."

Suddenly her mom whirled around. "Oh, dear me. Sorry, Ryker, I think I left my manners down the mountain or something." Mom set her bundle on the counter and hurried over to Ryker and hugged him. "It's so good to see you again."

* * *

Ryker had never felt so awkward in his life. He knew this day would come, but he didn't know how Shelby's parents would react. After all, he'd left their daughter without telling her or them why. "Mrs. Davis, it's good seeing you again too." He returned her hug and whispered in her ear. "Thank you for the warm welcome."

He pulled back, and she nodded and smiled.

Letting her go, he turned his gaze to Shelby where it

locked and stayed for a good ten seconds or so. It would be so nice to be able to read her mind about the whole situation as he certainly couldn't ask if she was mad at him now for leaving her as he had the night before. Unfortunately, mental telepathy was not his strong suit, and she looked away before he could discern her thoughts.

"So, Ryker, tell us where you've been the last eighteen months." Mr. Davis's cool tone and his narrowed eyes told Ryker the man wasn't as happy as Mrs. Davis was to see him.

Ryker immediately felt like a prisoner in an interrogation room. All eyes were on him, and he fought not to twist and turn under the scrutiny.

Leave it to Mr. Davis to be blunt. He always had been, and Ryker had always loved him for it. One never had to guess as to how the man felt, which Ryker had admired until this very minute. Besides, he'd always treated Ryker like a son. Now it didn't feel that way at all.

"Listen, why don't I get dinner on the table and Ryker can tell us all about it then?" Shelby scurried to the kitchen before her dad had a chance to protest. That felt even worse.

Shelby's mom shed her coat and boots, slipped into a woman's pair of fur-lined, leather house slippers at the door, then hurried to join Shelby in the kitchen, leaving Ryker alone with Mr. Davis.

"What can I do to help?" Was the last thing Ryker heard Shelby's mom say before Mr. Davis came up to him and gripped his shoulder firmly.

"You'd better have a darn good reason why you left my daughter the way that you did." The man kept his voice low so as not to alert the women, and the darks of his eyes said if the reason wasn't good enough, there was about to be a brawl right in the middle of Shelby's living room.

However, Ryker refused to break eye contact with the man, he had too much respect for Mr. Davis to do that. Plus, he wanted to show him he wasn't intimidated by him at the same time. "I did."

"Well, I can't wait to hear it." Mr. Davis removed his hand from Ryker's shoulder, then took off his coat and boots, slipped his stocking feet into the pair of men's leather house slippers, and without another word to Ryker, he headed in to the kitchen.

Ryker noticed another pair of men's leather slippers there. They weren't there the other day when he'd come. He didn't want to presume they were for him, so instead of putting them on after he took his outer winter garments off, he plodded across the knotty pine floor toward the kitchen in his stocking feet.

Everyone pitched in to set the table. The whole time Mr. Davis kept eyeing him. He knew the man was curious, and he didn't blame him. If Ryker had a daughter and that happened to her, he'd want to know too.

With the table all set, everyone sat down.

The smell of roast beef and gravy filled the air, but he wasn't sure he'd be able to eat with all the knots tying off in his stomach.

"Dad, would you pray?"

"Sure will, kitten."

Everyone bowed their head, except him. His gaze landed on each person as his mind zinged.

What if the Davises didn't understand his reasons for leaving?

Or think it was good enough?

Would they throw him out?

"Amen."

Ryker slammed his eyes shut and echoed, "Amen," before opening them again.

Mr. Davis stared at him with eyes of steel. "Okay, I want to hear why you left our Shelby like you did."

"Dad!"

"Terry!"

Both Shelby and her mom said at the same time.

"Can't it wait until after we eat? Please?" Shelby shifted in her chair and shook her head.

"Yes, Terry, it can wait." Mrs. Davis stated, leaving no room for her husband to argue. "Right now, we're going to enjoy this delicious dinner Shelby has prepared for us."

Dinner went pretty well, considering.

Shelby asked about his ordeal with the stolen sleds, and he told her. Other than that, she and her mom kept the conversation off of Ryker and onto other things like the weather, the amount of snowfall they had here in Grand Lake, the lake itself, and on and on. Ryker wanted to hug the women who resembled each other in almost every way.

They both stood five-feet, five-inches tall.

Other than a few gray hairs, their hair color

matched.

The only real difference between the two besides their ages, was that Mrs. Davis's eyes were hazel, and Shelby's were a dark brown like her dad's.

Mr. Davis looked like one of those men on the TV commercials. His broad shoulders and tall frame could be quite intimidating at times.

When they all finished, Shelby pushed herself away from the table. "Shall we have desert in the living room?"

Everyone stood.

"I don't know about anyone else, kitten, but I'm stuffed. I'd rather have mine later, if you don't mind."

Shelby's gaze went to Ryker.

"I'm full too." Even though the roast beef, carrots, and potatoes tasted great, Ryker had to force them down because all during dinner his stomach wouldn't stop twisting into knots. He didn't want to have to force desert down too.

Everyone sat down in the living room near the fireplace.

Ryker debated on whether or not to sit on the couch at the far end of the living room or on the loveseat Shelby occupied. Mr. and Mrs. Davis had the two recliners. He knew if he sat on the couch, they'd think he was separating himself from them, and Mr. Davis was sure to think he was trying to avoid their talk. So, Ryker chose to sit next to Shelby on the loveseat.

"Okay, let's hear it."

Man, Mr. Davis didn't waste any time, that was for sure.

"Terry! You're making Ryker uncomfortable," Mrs. Davis scolded her husband.

"It's okay, Mrs. Davis. I don't blame him. I hurt his daughter, and he's only protecting her. I'd do the same thing if I was in his shoes."

Mr. Davis frowned as if he didn't believe him. Then out of nowhere he asked, "How come you don't seem to be upset over this, Shelby? Or as surprised to see Ryker as we are?"

"Dad, it's a long story." She crossed her leg toward Ryker and started shaking her foot. "Let's let Ryker explain, and then I'll tell you, okay?"

Her dad nodded but didn't look overly pleased.

Ryker tugged on the legs of his jeans and drew in a long breath. This was going to be a lot harder than he originally thought. He gathered his courage and plunged forward. "The reason I left the way I did, Mr. Davis, is because I thought I was dying."

"Dying!" Mrs. Davis gasped. The very same reaction her daughter had when he'd told her. Those two were so much alike it was downright uncanny.

"Yes, ma'am." He then proceeded to tell them the same thing he'd told Shelby, about his diagnosis, about why he didn't get a second opinion or treatment.

"Why didn't you suck it up like a man and tell Shelby instead of just calling her without any explanation?"

"Dad!"

"Terry!"

Mother and daughter both said it in unison again.

But Mr. Davis's steely eyes never left Ryker.

"You're right, Mr. Davis. I took the coward's way out. I apologize for that. But at the time I thought it the right thing to do. I knew if I told Shelby what the doctors had said that she would marry me anyway, and I wasn't going to let that happen."

"You're right. I would have," Ryker barely heard Shelby's words.

He turned his face toward her. Their eyes met. He wished her folks weren't in the room because he wanted to pull her into his arms and hold her and kiss away the melancholy he saw in her eyes.

"I don't understand. If you were diagnosed with a terminally ill cancer, how come," Mrs. Davis's gaze glanced away then came back up to him. "If you didn't have cancer, then what did you have?"

"Nothing. The lump wasn't malignant."

"How did you find that out?" Shelby's voice reached him from beside her.

"Well, I kept waiting to get worse, but after several months went by and nothing changed, I checked on the Internet and found several articles about how cancer, even today, is often misdiagnosed or not diagnosed at all. In fact, doctors believed that the most misdiagnosed cancer is lymphoma.

"That gave me hope, so I went to the nearest oncologist. He got copies of my records, and when he read the lab reports, because of the way they'd worded their findings, he ordered the sample to be retested. The results came back negative."

"How could something like that happen?" Shelby asked.

His focus went to her. "Several reasons. False positives. Pathology errors. My doctor said things like that happen all the time. He also explained how pathology technology needs to be improved."

"See, Terry, I told you Ryker had a good reason for leaving like he did." Mrs. Davis's faith in him touched Ryker deeply.

He shifted his attention to Mr. Davis. The knots in his stomach loosened when he noticed the hardness his eyes no longer remained. "I'm truly sorry for leaving like I did. I hope you understand now why I did it though."

Mr. Davis turned his focus onto his wife. He reached across the chair and took her hand. "I do, son. I probably would have done the same thing. I could never bear to see either one of my girls hurting." He looked back at Ryker. "I do wish you would have told us though and your folks. They were worried sick about you. We all could have helped you through this and supported you."

"Thank you, but at the time, I felt the best thing for everyone concerned was for me to leave. I didn't want any of you to go through what I had with Randy. Especially my parents. Once was enough for them."

"Don't you think you're leaving hurt them worse?"

Ryker rubbed the back of his head. "At that time, I didn't think about it that way. Honestly, I was too confused and too scared." The last words barely came out above a whisper. It was hard for him to admit that he'd been afraid. After all, men weren't supposed to show fear. If they did, it was considered a sign of weakness. That's what his grandpa had always told him anyway.

For several seconds the sound of the fireplace popping and cracking slipped into the stillness. Relief poured over him that no one said anything about his fears and weakness. Maybe Grandpa was wrong.

* * *

Shelby stared into the fire. All that time, she had never once thought about what Ryker was going through. She'd only thought of herself and how she had felt. Hearing Ryker admit he was afraid broke her heart. She'd always thought of him as strong and brave. He always protected her, defended her, and seemed to have it all together. But, he was human after all.

She reached for his hand. "I'm glad you came back, and that you're here now." Leather squeaked as she leaned over and kissed his cheek. Pine-scented aftershave floated up her nose.

"You don't seem as surprised to see him as we did, kitten. How come?" her dad asked once again.

Shelby pulled back and explained the search and rescue and the last few days. When she finished, her dad looked over at Ryker. "Well, you've had a couple of pretty good scares." He leaned forward and his gaze turned serious. "Now that you're back, I want to know what are you intentions are. Are you going to marry my daughter, or what?" A smirk quirked her dad's lips.

"Dad!" Shelby wanted to slink off the chair and out of the room. An image of Mr. Grinch doing something similar came to mind. Truth was, she wasn't sure she was ready to hear Ryker's answer to that question. While she completely understood his reasons and even thought them admirable, her heart and her head battled with trusting him again. Her heart said yes, her mind screamed no.

Eighteen long months she'd tried to figure out why he'd left her like he had. Often times, she wondered if it was something she had done or something she didn't do. The pain of his rejection still lingered in her heart and his explanation had done very little to ease that. Truth was, because of his abandonment, trust was now hard for her.

Not only did she struggle with trusting Ryker again, but even worse, God. Oh, sure, she went through the motions of being a Christian. She went to church, prayed, and talked about God, and even worshipped Him, but her heart was far from Him. She just couldn't wrap her mind around the fact that God had allowed her to go through all those months of pure torture, wondering if she wasn't good enough for Ryker or anyone else.

Just how did one get over something like that?

Chapter Eight

Early the next morning, Shelby stood at the stove scrambling the eggs. She'd barely gotten a wink of sleep. Some of the restlessness was from her conversation with Ryker, the other with trying to figure out if there really could be a place for Ryker in her future. When her dad had asked Ryker his intentions and if he was going to marry her, thank God her mom had stepped in and forced Dad to back off.

"Shelby, are you listening?"

"What? Oh, sorry, Mom. What did you say?"

"I asked if you wanted coffee or orange juice or both."

"Oh, um, both."

Her mom laid her hand on Shelby's arm. "Shelby, I know Ryker's being back here is both exciting and hard for you, and that you don't know what to do about it all. One thing you need to do, sweetie, is pray."

Shelby leaned her hip against the counter, snatched up a turkey sausage link, and bit off a chunk. Giving herself time to think of a response, she chewed slowly, then swallowed. "I did that before I told Ryker I'd marry him, and look where that got me." Frustration and anger came alongside her like two old friends.

"Shelby, you can't blame God for this."

"Why not, Mom? He could have stopped the whole

thing, but He didn't."

"Shelby, honey, do me a favor. Read the story about Joseph. And when you do, don't just read it. Stop and think about all that Joseph went through and especially the words *The Lord was with Joseph.* Promise me you'll do that, okay?"

"Okay." She had no clue why her mom wanted her to but she would.

"When you finish it, come talk to me about it, okay?"

She nodded. "It might be awhile. I have a lot going on over the next few days. Oh, and speaking of a lot going on, I hope you don't mind, but I invited the McIntyres over for dinner tomorrow night. Tomorrow is Friday, right?"

Her mom nodded.

"Mr. McIntyre wants to try and beat Dad at Monopoly." She bit into the sausage link her fingers still held.

Her mother groaned and glanced skyward. "This ought to be interesting. When those two get together and play Monopoly, they play as if they're really buying real estate and spending real money. It's not just a game to them, it's a competition. It's like watching two male egos going head-to-head to see who's the better businessman or something." Mom shook the spatula at her. "Did you hide the Monopoly?"

"No."

"Maybe we can throw it out or something."

"No can do. I already told Mr. McIntyre that I had it and that I knew where it was."

"What did you go and do that for?"

Shelby shrugged. "Momentary insanity?"

"I'll say." They giggled.

Her dad walked up behind her mother and put his arms around her and kissed her by her ear. "What are my two girls talking about in here?"

"Monopoly." Shelby burst out laughing.

At his confused frown, Shelby laughed harder and her mom joined her.

"Women." He shook his head. "Who can figure them out?"

Shelby shut the burner off and dumped the eggs into a bowl. Her mom grabbed the platter of turkey links and handed the plate of homemade hash browns to her father. They went to the table and sat down. After grace, everyone dived in.

"Pass me the orange juice if you would, kitten?"

Shelby handed her dad the pitcher of juice, then took a big bite of hash browns.

"So, do you think you'll marry Ryker if he proposes?"

Shelby sucked in a breath. A piece of potato followed. She coughed and hacked until the piece dislodged itself, then took a drink of her juice.

"Terry, we are not discussing this. Leave Shelby be about Ryker. And Ryker too. They are adults. They can make that decision for themselves."

He raised his hands in surrender. "Okay, okay. I'm only asking because I like that boy. Always have. What he did wasn't right, but I sure understand why he did it now. That had to be hard on him."

Hard on him? What about me? But Shelby kept those questions to herself.

"So, what's on the agenda for today?" Shelby wanted to hug her mom for changing the subject.

"I'd like to go for a ride. You still have machines, don't you, kitten?"

"Sure do. Four of them."

"Good. Why don't you see if Ryker would like to come with us and let's go see if we can find some elk?" At her mom's scowl, he quickly added, "If you want to that is."

She wasn't sure she wanted to spend so much time with Ryker yet. She still had to sort things out in her heart and mind. Being around him so much would just complicate things even more. "The truth is, I have a deadline I've got to work on. But you and Mom go on ahead. You can take my truck and trailer. The machines are all fueled and ready to go."

"When's your deadline?"

"February 20th."

"Oh, you have plenty of time then. C'mon, kitten. Come and go with us."

She knew when her dad got his mind on something, nothing would change it, so she might as well just give in and work late tonight. "Okay, I'll go. But we don't need to bother Ryker. I'm sure he has to work at his shop."

"Nope, I already asked him."

"What? Seriously? Dad, tell me you didn't. When?"

"This morning when I called him."

"This morning? What time did you call him?" She

glanced at the clock on the microwave. 8:07. "It's barely after eight now."

"Called him right before we sat down to eat. He said he'd love to go." Dad slathered a chunk of soft butter onto his wheat toast, smiling the whole time.

"What would you have done if I said no," Shelby mumbled around the mound of hash browns and sausage she shoved into her mouth to keep from saying more.

"What was that, kitten?" her dad asked, looking all innocent.

Innocent? Humpft. Nothing innocent about it. More like meddlesome. "Nothing, nothing at all." It amazed Shelby how her dad went from being upset with Ryker to treating him like a son in the flash of a snowmobile light. Then again, her father had always wanted a son, and he'd always loved Ryker as if he were his own flesh and blood. If she and Ryker married, he'd finally have the son he always wanted.

Where would that leave her in her daddy's life?

After all, growing up that's all she ever heard about was how much her father wanted a son. Even though her dad doted on her, she never felt like she was good enough because she wasn't a boy. A boy who would play baseball and watch football games on TV with her dad. Oh, sure she done all those things and had even helped him restore his Model A car. Still, she knew she wasn't a replacement for the son he always wanted and never could have. Would Ryker?

As they finished breakfast, the more she thought about things, the more she stewed about them. She couldn't believe her dad had taken it upon himself to invite Ryker without even asking her first. Shelby loved her dad, but how dare he do that? She wasn't a child anymore. So when would he stop treating her like one?

* * *

More snow had fallen the night before. At least four more inches. Today would be a good day for snowmobiling. With Jeff's help, Ryker loaded four of Ryker's best machines, including the two those men had tried to steal. Well, they wouldn't be stealing anymore. Thanks to the three Colorado State Patrol and the big wrecker with a plow on the front that had showed up. Ryker followed behind them, careful to stay out of their way as they followed the thieves' tracks up the same road where Ryker had gotten stuck.

About a mile up the winding, narrow road was a log cabin, obviously someone's summer place, and the two men were holed up there.

The patrol surrounded the place and the men came out with their hands up. They were arrested and were now sitting in jail.

Ryker turned carefully into Shelby's drive. It blessed him that Mr. Davis had called to invite him. The man had sure done a 360 after he'd explained why he'd left.

Ryker still couldn't believe Mr. Davis had asked him what his intentions were toward Shelby. Oh, he understood Mr. Davis's reasoning behind wanting to know, but he and Shelby needed time to figure that out first.

Ryker already knew what he wanted. He wanted her, all of her, ring on the finger, bells in the background, but he wasn't sure Shelby wanted the same thing. Even though she had kissed him and had appeared to enjoy having him around, a barrier still stood between them. Not on his part, but on Shelby's. He didn't blame her. After all, if the situation was reversed, he wasn't sure how he'd feel either. Oh, it's easy for someone to say what they'd do until the noose was around their own neck. Then it was a whole different matter altogether.

Just because his reasons for leaving were genuine and he completely believed at the time he'd done the right thing, seeing how his leaving had affected Shelby, he wasn't so sure now. Truth be known, either way was hurtful.

What he did know was that he loved her more now than ever, and he wanted to make her his wife. But he also knew it would take time and patience to tear down the wall she'd built around her heart and to remove the uncertainty and lack of trust he saw in her eyes. *If* that ever happened. And it was a pretty big if.

The sidewalks were already cleared as Ryker walked up the stone pathway to Shelby's front door.

He could hear Max barking inside, and within seconds the dog's nose pressed up against the window, fogging it up. Today was even colder than the day before. But that didn't bother Ryker. He loved the cold. He rang the doorbell and waited for someone to answer. It didn't take long and Mr. Davis opened the door.

"Come on in. We just finished breakfast." Mr. Davis stepped out of the way and Ryker stepped inside.

"Morning," Mrs. Davis greeted him.

"Morning, Mrs. Davis. Morning, Shelby."

Standing at the kitchen island counter with her back to him, Shelby gave a short wave and didn't even bother looking at him.

Oh oh. Not good. Not good at all. Something was wrong.

"Have you eaten?" Mrs. Davis asked.

"I have. Thank you."

"Oh, okay." Mrs. Davis turned back to the counter and loaded stuff into their backpacks. "We're just gathering some supplies to take along today, and then we're ready to head out the door."

"I brought some supplies too. And four sleds. We can all go in my rig, if you'd like. What do you say, Shelby?"

"Whatever everyone else wants to do is fine with me." She didn't bother to turn around when she spoke.

Was it really? he wanted to ask.

"Don't pay any attention to her. She's been like this since breakfast." Mr. Davis spoke low enough that only Ryker heard him.

Ryker wondered what had happened at breakfast.

Minutes later, they loaded up in Ryker's pickup. Mr. Davis sat up front with Ryker, and Shelby and her mom sat in the backseat.

The whole drive up to the trailhead to Gravel Mountain Mr. Davis talked. No one got a word in edgewise. Ryker could hardly wait to ask Shelby what was wrong. He'd glanced in his rear-view mirror and got a glimpse of her sitting with her arms crossed looking out the window. How she could see anything with it fogged over was beyond him.

He pulled into the exact spot where the search and rescue had set up the night he'd gotten lost. A few rigs were parked here, but not as many as there usually were. On the weekends this place was packed and you were lucky if you found a spot.

Before everyone dressed in their snowmobile garb, Ryker made sure everyone had a beacon, probe, and GPS strapped on under their coats. He also made sure they each had their cell phones and a collapsible shovel in both their backpack and sleds in case they needed to dig out.

Shelby informed him she wasn't stupid, that she had already seen to all of that, just like she always did when she rode anywhere or went on a search and rescue mission.

Boy was she touchy today.

Satisfied that everyone had the right safety equipment, they unloaded the machines.

"Nice machine. I've been wanting one of these." Mr. Davis climbed on one of the Polaris RMK PRO 800's.

Ryker brought four of the six he owned because he knew Shelby wanted to ride one.

He trekked through the deep snow and made his way to her. "Are you okay?"

She turned her face up to him. "Fine. Why?"

"You don't act like it. Your dad said you've been this way since breakfast. What gives?"

"I'll tell you what gives." She glanced over at her

dad and lowered her voice. "I'm not a child, and I can make my own decisions." Shelby brushed past him and claimed a sled.

Ryker scratched his forearm. Where had that come from? Who said she was a child? Not him, that's for sure. Shelby was all woman with all the right curves in all the right places.

Ryker let out a long breath of air. Women. Who could ever figure them out? A shrug, and then he shoved his head gear on, and mounted his sled. Ryker made sure he had his GPS with the new batteries he installed earlier that morning, along with his fully charged cell phone in the pockets of his snowmobile suit. Fish would fly before he let a repeat of what happened to him a couple of weeks ago ever happen again. He still suffered from some of the effects of hypothermia, but for the most part, he felt pretty good.

With their backpacks loaded they headed out.

For hours they rode the trails and wove through the pine and aspen trees. Fresh powder made for great snowmobiling. Everyone but Shelby seemed to be enjoying themselves. By now Ryker's nerves were catching up to him. What was wrong her? *Lord, help me get Shelby alone so I can clear the air and find out exactly what is wrong and what she meant earlier.*

* * *

The sunshiny weather and fresh powder couldn't get much better for riding, and yet Shelby couldn't get into it. Misery hung over her like a black umbrella.

During the ride, her dad rode close to Ryker, leaving her and her mother to follow them. Not that she minded that, but seeing them together reminded her of how her dad always acted when Ryker was around. It was if Shelby were invisible.

Was she jealous? Or was her being bugged and bent out of shape due to that old feeling of never measuring up, of not being good enough because she wasn't a boy? Weird how that never once bothered her during the eighteen months that Ryker had been gone. Of course, her dad didn't have him around to dote on either.

Ack! She hated feeling like this. Gunning her machine, she took off in the opposite direction of them. In the wide open space she made figure eights. Each curve, she stood on one leg the other leg she knelt on the seat while she leaned her machine into the curve. Snow sprayed behind her in the shape of an opened paper fan. Around and around she went, when she tired of that, she headed up into the trees, making sure she kept an eye on everyone so that they all stayed in the same vicinity.

All of sudden, she hit a blind flat spot and her machine went nose first into the bank on the other side. Great. She shut the sled off, climbed off the sled, and ended up in snow way past her knees.

She slid her backpack off, grabbed her shovel out of it, and put it together. She removed her helmet and set it out of the way and turned it upside down.

One shovel full at a time she dug and tossed the snow off to the side.

The roar of machines neared, but she ignored them and kept on digging.

"Hey, watch where you're throwing that stuff."

She turned to see Ryker's face mask covered with powder. "Sorry," she said even though a part of her wanted to laugh at how comical he looked standing there with clumps of powdery snow plastered on his mask and down the front of his snowmobile jacket.

He removed his helmet and laid it on the seat his machine. "Let me do that." He reached for her shovel.

She yanked it away. "I can do it," she bit out. What was wrong with her biting his head off like that?

Ryker held up his hands. "Whoa, I didn't say you couldn't. I was just going to help you. I know how tiring it can get."

"What for a woman?" She shoveled harder, sending even more snow out.

"Ryker and Shelby have this under control, honey. Why don't we ride around in the clearing until they finish?"

Shelby knew what her mom was doing. She was leaving them alone so she and Ryker could work this out. Whatever this was.

"Shelby needs help. We can do that after I help Ryker get her sled out."

Help Ryker get her sled out? *Seriously?* Didn't her dad think she could do anything? She'd been stuck a million times and a million times she gotten herself out. Curtailing her anger, she spoke calmly, "I can get it, Dad. I'm not helpless. I do this all the time."

"What, get stuck?" It was meant as a joke, but it hurt nonetheless.

"Ha. Ha. Very funny. You and Mom and Ryker go

ahead. I got myself into this mess, I can get myself out."
She put her back to all three of them and continued to
dig. Even though she worked out almost daily, her arms
ached at the numerous shovelful of snow she tossed
aside.

In mid-toss, a strong arm banded around hers.
"Shelby, stop."

Shelby whirled as best as she could in the deep
snow. "Stop what? Being a girl?"

Ryker balked as if he'd been slapped. "What is
wrong with you today, Shelby? I've never seen you like
this before."

"I'll tell you what's wrong." She jammed the shovel
into the snow and glared up at him. "I may not have been
born a boy, but I can do just as much as any man can."

"Whoa. Where'd that come from?" He frowned.
"You're not making any sense."

"You wouldn't understand. You're a man." She
yanked her arm from his grasp, jerked her shovel out of
the snow, and continued digging.

From the corner of her eye, she watched Ryker get
the shovel from his backpack. Without another word, he
helped her. Guilt pounced on Shelby. The man didn't
deserve her anger.

Or did he? After all, her dad always accused her of
being weak as a kitten. That's why he called her kitten.
All of a sudden, she hated that nickname. Ryker believed
the same thing about her too, that she wasn't strong
enough to deal with his dying.

Ack! She hated feeling like she wasn't good enough
and never would be. She jammed the shovel hard into the

ground and hit a rock. Pain bolted through her shoulder. "Ow!"

Ryker was at her side in an instant. "What's the matter? Are you hurt?"

"No." *Only my pride.* Earlier she told herself she wasn't a child, well she was sure acting like one now. No wonder her dad still treated her like one. Remorse slipped over her. She brought her gaze up to Ryker. "I'm sorry. I shouldn't have taken my frustration out on you."

"I don't get it. Why are you so frustrated? Did I say or do something to make you feel that way? If you didn't want me along today, you just had to tell me. You know that, don't you?"

"What do you mean I don't want you along? Where'd you get that idea?"

"Well, you've ignored me ever since I got to your house. It doesn't take a genius to figure that one out." He draped his hand over the shovel sticking out of the snow.

"Don't mind me, okay? I'm being silly."

"How do you know you're being silly?"

"Because I do. Now, let's get me out of here so we can head on back to the truck." She turned to start shoveling again, but Ryker clutched her arm.

Peering over his shoulder, he turned his head back around, pulled her face to his, and kissed her. His lips were wet and warm and exhilarating. Not giving a second thought to her parents and what they would think if they saw them kissing, she leaned into him and parted her mouth, her lips played with his.

Ryker responded to her every move and even had a few of his own. Shelby clung to him. Oh how she wanted this, needed this. She couldn't help herself. Nor at the moment, did she want to. Right now, all she wanted to do was live the fantasy that she was good enough for Ryker. She kissed him like she'd never kissed him before, with passion, desire, and love.

From this moment on, she would strive to prove to both him and her father that she wasn't a weak woman. That she was worthy of their love.

Chapter Nine

All the way back to Shelby's house, Ryker relived that kiss. He had no idea what Shelby tried to prove, but whatever it was, she'd more than succeeded. Her kiss had gone all the way through him. Good thing they weren't alone, or he wasn't sure what would have happened. In the past, they'd always avoided those types of intimate kisses, knowing what they could lead to. They were saving themselves for their wedding night, a gift to each other. Had they been alone, ashamed to admit it, that kiss might have changed everything. *Thank you, Lord, for protecting me and Shelby from sinning against you.*

"What do you say, Ryker?"

Ryker turned his glance toward Mr. Davis. "About what?"

"Weren't you listening, son?"

"Sorry, sir. My mind was somewhere else."

"I'll bet it was, and I'll bet I know exactly where it was." He waggled his graying eyebrows.

"Dad!"

"Ha! I was right."

"Terry, leave them alone." From the back seat, Mrs. Davis swatted her husband's shoulder.

"Hey, I remember when I used to kiss you like that."

"You still do." She giggled.

"Dad! Mom! Seriously?"

Ryker glanced in the rear view mirror.

Shelby slunk down lower, crossed her arms over chest, and rolled her eyes.

Ryker chuckled.

"It's not funny," Shelby said.

"Yes it is." Ryker laughed and Mr. Davis joined him.

"Will you two behave yourselves?" Mrs. Davis scolded, but humor laced her voice.

How he'd missed these people. They always had such a good time together, joking, laughing, and just being themselves. It was great being with them again. He hoped and prayed that one day he'd have a marriage like theirs. Even after thirty years, they still held hands, kissed, and did special things for each other.

"Okay, I'll quit teasing them. Are you going to stay for supper, Ryker?" Mr. Davis asked.

"Supper?"

"Yeah, Shelby asked if you wanted to stay for supper this evening and play some cards or something."

"Can't this evening. But thanks for the invite." In the rear-view mirror he glanced at Shelby again. Was it his imagination or did she appear disappointed? That was a good sign. Wasn't it? "So, what time tomorrow, Shelby?"

"Tomorrow? Oh, yeah, tomorrow's Friday night. I told the McIntyre's we'd have dinner at six. So, any time before then is fine."

"Do you need me to bring anything?"

"Nope, just yourself."

He nodded, and minutes later he pulled into Shelby's drive.

Everyone got out, and Ryker helped carrying stuff into the house. When everything was finished, standing at the front door he said, "See you all tomorrow."

"Looking forward to it." Mr. Davis shook Ryker's hand. For his age, his grip was solid and definitely not wimpy.

"I'll walk you out." Shelby followed him out to his truck.

Ryker looked over at the big picture window. Mr. and Mrs. Davis stood there with their arms around each other, watching, and smiling. Ryker raised his hand and gave a short wave. As soon as he did, they backed away and the curtain drew shut. Their shadows came together in a kiss. Ryker envied them.

"You want help cleaning the machines?" Shelby asked from behind him. Wisps of white followed her words.

The wind picked up, making it go from nice to chilly. Clouds rolled in, hiding most of the sun.

A strand of her hair blew across her face. He reached over and tucked it behind her ear. His finger trailed down her cheek and over her lips. Lips that were cool and soft.

Shelby gazed up at him. "So kiss me already. I'm getting cold."

"Well, I can remedy both of those." He pulled her into his arms as close to him as their coats would allow, hoping the heat from his body would spread to hers to help warm her up.

He lowered his head, holding her gaze as he did.

Slowly, he descended.

Right before he reached her lips, his eyelids lowered.

A quick peck on her cheek and he yanked his head up. "Night, Shelby." He turned to go, but she grabbed his arms and yanked him back around.

"Oh, no, you don't. You're not getting off that easy." She pulled his head down to hers and kissed him long and hard.

He didn't know about her, but he wasn't cold at all. In fact, he was smothering, and it had nothing to do with the weather.

Again, he had to stop her from kissing him like that even though he really didn't want to. He raised his head. Keeping his lips close to hers, he whispered, "I love you, Shelby." Fearing her reaction, he quickly set her from him, yanked his truck door open and climbed inside. "Sweet dreams."

He knew his would be.

* * *

Late that evening, after writing over six-thousand words of her novel, Shelby climbed into bed and pulled her favorite color comforter under her chin. She stared at the ceiling for several minutes until her eyes drifted shut.

Ryker's face slipped into view, and she thought about their kisses today. She had longed to show him through her kiss how much she loved him and how deserving she was of his love. That she wanted him to love her. Yet when he whispered that he loved her, she'd panicked.

Confusion scraped across her mind.

How could she love him and want his love so badly, and yet at the same time be so deathly afraid to receive it and to offer her love back to him again?

"God, please help me. I'm so afraid. Afraid of not being good enough. Afraid that I did something wrong and that is really why Ryker left. Sure he said it was because he thought he was dying and didn't want me to watch him go through it, but love doesn't run when things get rough. It stays. Yet Ryker didn't. So what does that say about his love toward me?"

Shelby glanced at the clock. 10:15. Knowing Hailey would still be up, she snatched the phone off her night stand and called her.

"Hey, girl, what's up?" Hailey's cheerful voice greeted her.

"You sound chipper."

"I am. Jeff's here," she whispered.

"Oh. How's that going?"

"Great. Jeff, stop that." She giggled. "I'm trying to talk to Shelby.

"Tell her hi." Shelby heard him say in the background.

"Tell him hi for me."

"Shelby says hi back. Now, be a good boy and go fetch us some popcorn while I talk to Shelby, okay?"

"You're every wish is my command." His voice in the background wasn't very loud, but Shelby heard it just the same.

"Silly man." Hailey chuckled. "So, tell me what's up. You never call me this late unless something's bothering you. So spill."

"I've been seeing Ryker again."

"You have?" Shelby could just see her friend sitting up and suddenly all ears. "And...?" She dragged out the word 'and'.

"And, it's going great..."

"Uh-oh, I hear a but in there somewhere."

"Well, it's just that, even though I still love him, I'm scared to death to love him."

"Whoa. You lost me, girl. What do you mean?"

"Well, the truth is, I'm afraid I'm not good enough for him."

"What do you mean you're not good enough? You're one of the sweetest, most generous, kindest ladies I know. You're successful in your writing career. You train search and rescue dogs. You've helped rescue several people, saving their lives in the process."

"Yes, but I think I did the whole search and rescue thing because men usually do that, and well, Daddy always wished he had a son."

"You may not be the son your dad always wanted, Shelby, but your dad adores you. Anyone who has eyes and ears knows that."

"I know, but, it's those little things that he says."

"Like what?"

"Oh, you know. 'If you were a boy we could go hunting together.'"

"You hunt."

"Yes, but there's always something. I keep trying to

be the boy he never got, but I just feel like all my trying isn't working."

"So. Stop trying."

"What do you mean?"

"Shelby, listen to me. You can't change the fact that you were born a girl. You can't change the fact that your dad wanted a son. But what you can change is how you react to that."

"I don't understand."

"Shelby, I love you, you know that, right?"

Uh-oh. Whenever Hailey said that, it meant Shelby was going to hear something that wasn't easy to hear, but always worthwhile hearing. "Yes."

"Stop it. Okay? Stop trying to be someone you're not. What is it you want to do?"

"Write."

"You're doing that."

"Be a girl. I hate hunting. I hate fishing. And honestly, I hate football."

"I thought you loved football."

"I thought I did too. But honestly, I can't stand the sound of it even. I only watch it to please my dad. To be accepted by him. I think Dad wants me to marry Ryker just so he can have a son."

"Whoa. Where'd that come from?"

"The way he acted today and yesterday. Last night he was all up in Ryker's face about leaving me. After Ryker explained why he left, then it was like I no longer existed."

"Are you jealous of Ryker?"

Shelby paused and thought about that for a moment.

"Maybe." She scrunched her nose as if the words stunk. "I think so."

"So what are you going to do about that?"

"I don't know. But if I don't get a grip on this, I'm afraid I will push Ryker away a second time."

"You didn't push him away the first time. He chose to leave."

"But what if it was because he thought I was too weak and he didn't want a weak wife?"

"Okay, hang on, back up, girlfriend. Tell me why he said he left."

Shelby told her the whole story.

"And you think he left because you were too weak to handle it? Girl, I say he loved you so much he couldn't bear to see you suffer."

"Really?" Hope kissed the inside of her heart.

"Yes, really. Now stop all this nonsense about you not being good enough and about you being weak. And stop doing things you hate just to get your dad's approval. Trust me, girl, he loves you very much."

Shelby hoped Hailey was right. "Thanks, Hailey. Listen, girl, I've kept you from Jeff long enough. Love you."

"Love you too. And remember, stop it!"

Shelby giggled. "I'll try."

"No! Don't try. Do it! If you don't, I'm going to come over there and smack you around."

"Yeah right, you, who wouldn't hurt even a pesky spider, smack me around. Um huh. If I believed that, then I'd believe that ducks hate water. Not! Night, Hailey. Tell Jeff goodbye for me."

"Will do."

Shelby ended the call. She felt a lot better. She now knew what she needed to do. "Father God, help me to accept me for who I am, the Shelby that you created me to be. I know you have a plan and a purpose for each person's life. And if you had wanted me to be a boy, you would have made me one. But you didn't. Now help me to accept that fact, and please help my dad to, too. And Lord, I know this sounds terrible, but please don't let Ryker take my place with Daddy. Amen."

* * *

On Friday night, Ryker had a great time with the Davises and the McIntyre's and of course with Shelby. It was a hoot watching Mr. McIntyre and Mr. Davis battling to see who could win at Monopoly. After Ryker had lost, he went in the living room and sat down with the women.

Today was Saturday, and he was on his way to pick up Shelby for the benefit fund-raiser he was hosting.

When he arrived, he hurried to the door and rang the bell.

Mrs. Davis opened it. "Come on in. Shelby's almost ready."

He stepped inside and gave Mrs. Davis a hug. Mr. Davis sat in the recliner near the fireplace reading a newspaper. He folded it and set it on his lap, then removed his black framed reading glasses. "Evening, son."

"Evening. How are you, sir?"

"Great. Just enjoying a nice warm fire and being with those that I love."

"Nothing better than that. Oh, speaking of loved ones. My parents are flying back from Hawaii in a few days and would love to see you guys."

"It'll be good to see them again. Don't see much of them since we moved down the mountain."

"Hi, Ryker."

Ryker turned toward the sound of Shelby's voice.

Woo wee! Shelby's sandy-blonde hair was pulled up in some fancy hairdo with curly strands hanging on the side and down her sleek neck. She wore a black floor length gown with a split that went a few inches above her knee, revealing one very shapely leg. Those black heels made that leg really stand out.

The dress gathered at her waist, showing how tiny it was. One shoulder was covered with a long sleeve that looked like some kind of heavy lace material and the other shoulder and arm was bare. The plain truth was, she looked hot.

"You can stop staring now."

Mr. Davis and his bluntness. This was one time Ryker didn't appreciate it. Heat raced up Ryker's neck and into his face.

Shelby strolled up to him. "You look nice. A black tux definitely becomes you."

"That black dress becomes you too. You look beautiful, Shelby." He couldn't have stopped his lips from curling upward even if he tried.

She smiled, her white teeth sparkled and so did her eyes.

"Shall we go?" He offered her his arm.

She wove her hand through his arm. "Lead the way."

He said goodbye to Mr. and Mrs. Davis and led her to the door. She removed her full-length coat from off the back of the chair near the door and Ryker helped her into it.

"Be home before midnight."

"Dad," Shelby dragged out. "I'm not sixteen anymore. Besides, what do you think I'm going to do, turn into a pumpkin or something?"

"Who knows, you just might." Mrs. Davis stood next to her husband, her hip settled against his chair and her hand rested on his shoulder.

"You two are something else, you know that?" Shelby shook her head.

"We do, but you love us." Mrs. Davis winked.

"Yes, I do. Good night."

Ryker took that as his cue to leave. He opened the door and as soon as they stepped outside, he swept Shelby into his arms.

"What are you doing?"

"Carrying you."

"I can see that. Why?"

"Because I want to."

"Oh, okay." She looped her arms around his neck.

He didn't tell her that he was carrying her because even though the walkway was cleared of snow, those heels would be like ice skates on the ice-packed surface. He only hoped and prayed he didn't slip and fall with her.

Half an hour later, they arrived at his folk's lodge. Ryker pulled up next to the door. One of the four valets he'd hired for the evening opened Shelby's door and his. He tossed the keys to him and hurried around to Shelby's side. Arm-in-arm they headed inside. He didn't carry her here because the driveway and sidewalk were heated and therefore there was no danger of her slipping and falling.

They stepped inside and Shelby's mouth fell open. "Oh, Ryker, it's beautiful. Looks like something out of a Christmas movie or something." She gazed up at him. "You did a fabulous job." Pride pranced through those chocolate eyes of hers, and Ryker's chest swelled.

He glanced around, trying to see it all through her eyes.

Wrapped in silver garland with giant red bows, the log ceiling beams and rails looked pretty festive.

Dead center of the windowed wall stood a sixteen-foot Christmas tree decorated to the hilt with tons of colored lights and sparkling glass ornaments of various colors. A large, silver, northern-star treetop twinkled in tune to Joy to The World.

Tables were spread out all across the large room except for in one corner. That's where the band and the dance floor were.

White linen cloths with shorter red and green ones were draped over each of the tables in the room. Fresh floral centerpieces with pine boughs, red and white roses, and shiny Christmas balls and beads sat in the center of each one.

The room looked great, and he couldn't be more proud. He only wished his folks could have been here for this, and that Shelby's folks would have accepted his invitation to come too. Mr. and Mrs. Davis sent a sizeable donation, saying they just wanted to relax and that they'd attended enough charity balls and Christmas parties down the mountain.

Rows and rows of tables loaded with donated items for people to bid on lined the front of the room. The people of Grand County had been very generous. Extreme gratitude to them drifted over him. Search and rescue was truly an excellent cause.

Voices of people chattering rose above the Christmas tune *White Christmas* the band now played softly.

The scent of pine and citrus filled the air, mingled with roasted turkey and prime rib.

"Shelby!"

Ryker panned the crowd-filled room to see who had hollered Shelby's name.

Hailey, dressed in a short green sparkly gown bustled toward them with Jeff in tow.

When they reached them, Hailey hugged Shelby first and then threw her arms around Ryker. "Wow. You sure look a lot better than the last time I saw you. Good to see you again."

"Good to see you again too."

"Jeff." Ryker extended his hand toward his friend.

"Hey, buddy. Long time no see."

"Yeah right. I just saw you about two hours ago."

Jeff shrugged and grinned.

"Looks like a pretty good turnout," Shelby said from beside him, her eyes taking in the room.

"Sure does."

"C'mon, you two. We saved you guys a seat." Hailey snatched Shelby's arm and dragged her away.

"Guess we'd better follow, huh?" Jeff attention wasn't on Ryker, it was on the women's retreating forms.

Ryker didn't blame him. He rather liked the view himself. Shelby's view, that was. "You go on ahead. Tell Shelby I'll be there in a minute. I need to greet my guests." He had wanted her by his side when he did, but Hailey had taken off with her before he had a chance to say anything.

Ryker went about the room, welcoming and thanking the people for coming. Many of them he knew, but many he didn't.

Every so often, he glanced over at Shelby. She was busy chatting with Hailey and Jeff, but every once in a while their gazes met.

Satisfied that he'd made the rounds, he strode over to Shelby. He sat down, and Shelby immediately reached for his hand. "Glad you could join us." She winked at him and his heart winked in response.

He leaned toward her. "Sorry, I didn't mean to leave you by yourself, but I didn't have much choice. Hailey whisked you away, or I would have had you join me while I greeted my guests."

"Sure is a nice turnout." She glanced around the room. "Everything sure looks nice." Her eyes came to his. "When did you find time to do all this?"

"Most of it had been arranged for quite some time. The final arrangements I did on the weekend and evenings."

"Looks like a lot of people are bidding on the donations."

Ryker turned in his chair and looked at the donation tables. People dressed in simple clothing and finery alike were jotting down their bids.

His caterer strolled up to his table wearing a black and white uniform pantsuit pressed to perfection. The rest of her staff wore the same. "Every thing's ready, Mr. Anderson."

"Thank you, Margaret."

Ryker excused himself and headed to the stage. When the band finished playing *Jingle Bell Rock*, he motioned for them to stop. The lead singer handed him the microphone. "May I have your attention please?"

The noise slowly died down and all eyes went to him.

"Thank you all for coming this evening. As you know search and rescue is a great cause. If it wasn't for them, I probably wouldn't be here today. As you have already seen, we have some wonderful items for you to bid on. Please be generous to this cause, so that we can keep saving and rescuing those that need it. There's food and beverages set up, so please help yourself. Have fun and bid high. Thank you."

A round of applause filled the room.

Ryker stepped off the stage and made his way to Shelby. "Let's get something to eat. I'm starving."

"Me too."

He helped her from the chair and looped her hand through his. Whispers and curious stares followed them as they made their way to the food tables, but he'd expected that. Most of the people here knew that he and Shelby had been engaged. And most also knew how that had ended.

Shelby pressed tighter against him.

His gaze went down to her.

Her shoulders were rigid, and though she held her face straight ahead, her eyes darted left and right.

Ryker leaned down and whispered near her ear. "Don't let them bother you, Shelby."

She looked up at him. "This is so awkward. I hadn't even thought about how it would be until now. Almost everyone here knows you dumped me."

He stopped and took her hands in his. "Come on, Shelby, I didn't dump you. I left. There's a big difference. I know to you there probably isn't, but trust me, there is. Now, just hold that pretty little head of yours up high, and let's go get something to eat."

She nodded even though she didn't look overly convinced.

Ryker offered up a quick prayer for her. It was clear the hurt he'd caused. Less clear was if she could ever truly forgive him for that.

When they finished filling their plates and grabbing a cup of eggnog and bottled water, they went back to their seats. Jeff and Hailey were huddled together talking and laughing.

"You better get something to eat before it's all gone," Ryker told them.

They gazed up at him. "Thanks."

"Don't let him rush you. There's enough food there

to feed the entire town of Grand Lake."

They nodded, then went back to talking. Whatever they were saying must be good because they acted as if they were the only two people in the room. If Ryker wasn't mistaken, he'd bet there would be a wedding announcement coming soon.

* * *

Shelby was so glad to be back at the table. Everyone staring at them as she and Ryker walked by made her want to slink out of the room. Funny, she'd seen a lot of those same people in town and around the county but tonight was different. Tonight she was with Ryker, her ex-fiancé. Her focus shifted to him.

He looked great in his black tux. His broad shoulders and trim waist filled it out nicely. It hadn't gotten past Shelby's notice that he had on a powder blue shirt, her favorite color. That particular color brought out the blue in his blue-gray eyes. Tonight, he had even shaved the stubbles from his face. Truth be known, she liked those stubbles. They made him look ruggedly handsome. Tonight, however, he looked quite debonair.

Shelby and Ryker feasted on jumbo shrimp cocktails, stuffed mushrooms, baked potatoes, salad, prime rib, and barbequed chicken skewers. Each time she tried to talk to Ryker, someone would come up to the table and talk to him, telling him what a great job he'd done. Watching him interact with people from all walks of life and seeing how gracious he was to them, and how well he handled them all, sent warmth and joy over

Shelby.

Several of them spoke to her as well.

As strange as it sounded, being here with Ryker felt right.

Yet her fear of being abandoned again kept resurfacing. That fear kept her going around in circles, chasing the yes I can trust him with the no I can't. Right now, she was leaning more toward the yes I can.

Tired of sitting, Shelby stood and so did Ryker. All evening the band had played a mixture of Christmas, country and the oldies. The beginning of *Unchained Melody* drifted from them. Shelby looked over at Ryker, hoping he would ask her to dance to her favorite song.

"Please excuse me, Mr. Belmar."

"Oh, sure." Mr. Belmar turned his round face toward Shelby and smiled. "It's nice to see you two together again. God has finally answered our prayers."

Shelby forced her eyes not to widen. To think that Mr. Belmar, a wealthy tycoon had been praying for her and Ryker sent shock waves whooshing over her. "Thank you, Mr. Belmar." She hooked her arm through Ryker's and gazed up at him lovingly.

"You're welcome. Now, you two had better hurry before the song ends. I'll catch up to you later, Ryker. We'll talk about that expansion."

Mr. Belmar moved on to a small group of men.

Ryker took the moment to look down at her. "Shall we?"

"We shall."

This time Shelby ignored the stares. They reached the dance floor, and Ryker pulled her into his arms. She rested her head against his chest, and the two of them swayed back and forth to the music. Being in his arms this close brought so much joy to her heart. As the words to *Unchained Melody* drifted across them, Ryker leaned back. His movement caused her to raise her head.

Their gazes met and locked.

Ryker quietly sang along in that beautiful low voice of his. Each word he sang, he directed to her.

Shelby smiled up at him, touched by the love streaming from his eyes.

He continued to sing along, and at one point in the song, he ran the back of his fingers down her cheek and stroked it gently. Warm chills of love shivered through her. She, too, had missed and hungered for his touch.

The next set of words, Shelby knew he was asking her that question, she saw it in his blue eyes. Before she had a chance to answer if she was still his or not, he continued on, singing the chorus and hitting the high note in the song perfectly.

She needed his love too. Trust, would come, she was sure of it, but it would take work, and Ryker was worth it.

She'd listened to that song a million times, but the words held more meaning now than they ever had before.

The song ended, but Shelby didn't want to leave the shelter of Ryker's arms. However, the next song was a fast one, so she reluctantly took a step back in order to slip from his arms. She only made it one step before Ryker pulled her back to him and kissed her briefly on the lips, then he led her off the dance floor.

Back at the table, they were the only two people there now. Jeff and Hailey were off dancing.

She was glad to have this time alone with him. She'd never had a chance to ask him just where he had gone those eighteen months. The need to know now pressed in on her. "Ryker?"

"Yes, darling."

Darling? She hadn't heard him call her that in a very long time. Those words now wrapped around her like her favorite cashmere shawl, warming every inch of her spirit, soul, and body. She loved when he called her Darling. It made her feel cherished and loved. Like now. It gave her the courage to follow where her heart was leading. "Where were you those eighteen months you were gone?"

* * *

Whatever Ryker thought she was going to ask, that wasn't it. "Um, I went to Glendevey, Colorado."

"Glendevy? Where's that?"

"Exactly. It's near Jelm, Wyoming."

She tilted her head at him and sent him a questioning look.

"Jelm, Wyoming is about thirty-six miles from Laramie. And Glendevey is another eighteen miles from there."

"Why there?"

"I figured no one would look for me there."

"What did you do there?"

"I worked on a ranch."

"A ranch? You?"

Ryker laughed and tapped her chin back into place. "Yes. A guest ranch. It was actually a lot of fun. Hard work and long hours, but fun." Fun, if he didn't count his encounter with Tiffany Jones that was.

"So when did you know that you weren't going to die?" She picked up her water bottle and took a sip before setting it back on the table.

Ryker had hoped she wouldn't ask him that, but he might as well get it over with. He reached for her hands and held them. "About six months ago."

Shelby frowned. "You mean you've known for six months that you weren't going to die, and you didn't come back then?" She yanked her hands out of his and glared at him. "Why?"

"Because I didn't think you'd want to see me again after the way I left. In fact, I hadn't planned on coming back ever, but the more I thought about us, about you, the more I knew I had to come. When I saw the ad for the snowmobile shop in town for sale, I took that as a sign from God, and I knew I had to come back to see if there was any chance for us."

Shelby's eyes searched his. Doubt, confusion, and hurt filled those brown eyes of hers. He didn't blame her one bit, he'd be hurt and confused too.

"Shelby—" His cell phone chirped. *Oh, man, not now.* He pulled it out of his pocket and without looking at the number, he answered it. "This is Ryker."

He groaned. One hint of that voice, and his insides jumped to full alert. How had this crazy woman found him?

He turned away and spoke in as low of a tone as he could. "How'd you get this number? I told you to never call me again." He yanked the phone from his ear and poked *End* harder than he should have. Once again, it was a good thing he had bought the non-destructible phone or it would have broken for sure.

How had Tiffany found him? And why wouldn't the woman just leave him alone?

He looked back at Shelby. Arms crossed, she glared at him.

Oh, boy. How was he going to explain Tiffany?

His phone rang again, and he yanked back the sigh.

Shelby rose so fast she almost tipped her chair over and rushed out the front door.

Ryker jumped up and followed her. Outside the cold stripped his lungs of oxygen. He looked sideways hoping to see what direction Shelby went. He turned to go a different direction than the one he was facing and a woman stepped into his path. "Excuse me, ma'am, I—" His words died on his tongue. "You," he ground out, jaw clenched. "What are you doing here?"

Chapter Ten

Ryker yanked Tiffany by the arm and led her around the other side of the lodge. "How did you know I was here?"

"I had you followed, of course." She slithered her body up against his and spoke in a childish, nauseating purr—. "Didn't you miss me, darling? I missed you." She ran her finger across his cheek.

Ryker grasped her wrist. "Don't you ever touch me again."

Her villainous smile turned his stomach.

Suddenly her lips were on his, mashing into them with a ferocity that gripped the breath in his chest in a vice.

"So, this is what you were really doing the last eighteen months?"

Ryker yanked back and brushed his mouth across his tuxedo jacket sleeve as his stomach lurched and then plummeted.

Shelby stood there, arms crossed, anger scrawled across her face. The muscles in her neck stood out, and her eyes shot daggers of hatred toward him. Disgust and anger rounded her mouth and slanted her eyes.

Next to him, Tiffany pressed herself into his side and slipped her arm around his back. "I'm Tiffany, his fiancé. Who are you?"

* * *

Shelby couldn't believe her ears. Her stomach churned and bile rose up her throat. She swallowed hard. Tears stung the back of her eyes. A beautiful, shapely brunette who claimed to be Ryker's fiancée held out her hand for Shelby to shake. Like that would ever happen.

Ryker untangled himself from the woman. "Shelby she's—"

"I don't want to hear it."

He stepped toward her, but Shelby held up her hand. "Stop, right there. Don't you dare come near me or touch me ever again. I can't believe I trusted you and believed your lies. Well, I'll tell you one thing I won't make that mistake again. I never want to see you again." She whirled and her heels clicked with each step she took away from him. The tears wouldn't help anything, but they came anyway, and she hated what each one said about her.

"Shelby! Wait!"

She pushed herself harder until only the toes of her shoes were making contact with the pavement.

Cold pricked her lungs, and hurt pricked her heart.

When she ran out of pavement, she hiked up the lower part of her dress, and followed a path that a snowmobile had made up and into the snowpack beyond.

Bitter cold bit at her legs and feet.

Her heels slip-slid as she made her way over the hard-packed snow. Where she was going, she didn't know. The only clear thing was she had to get as far away from Ryker as possible. Everything else was lost in a complete blur.

Shivers from the cold and from what she'd just witnessed wracked her body.

She slipped and landed on her bare knee, hearing the skirt rip at the seam.

Stumbling back up to her feet, she kept running through the trees darting through them like a phantom ghost.

Ryker's voice followed her, calling to her as if he really believed she might stop long enough to listen to more of his lies.

She pressed herself further, blindly working her way further into the trees. Her burning lungs begged her to stop, but she refused to let that stop her.

Please, God, don't let Ryker catch up to me.

Her whole body ached from exertion and from the frigid cold, but right now she didn't care. The pain in her body was nothing compared to the agony ravishing in her heart.

Tears blurred her vision.

She stumbled her way through more trees, ones that were closer together, shielding her broken heart from the world.

Then through the blur, a strong hand banded around her arm.

"Leave me alone," she yelled. "Go away." She yanked her arm, trying to free herself from Ryker's grip, but he was too strong for her.

"Shelby, it's not what you think." His words came out in short pants.

She turned blazing eyes on him. "How do you know what I think?" she rasped. Streams of white rushed from her mouth. "Trust me, right now you don't even want to know what I think. I don't want to know what I think! Leave me alone!"

"Shelby, Tiffany is not my fiancée. She lied to you."

That yanked up her spirit, and she whirled on him, livid. "There's only one liar here, and it's you." Why wouldn't he just let her go?

"I did not lie to you. The woman is psycho. She's been stalking me for months. That's one reason I didn't come home right away. I was trying to get her off my tail. When she finally latched onto some other poor sap at the guest ranch, I thought I was safe, so I came home. Now, I realize that's what she wanted, to follow me here. The woman is crazy, Shelby. She's done nothing but sabotage me and everything I've tried to do for months. Everywhere I went, she turned up. She even trashed my room and shredded the pictures I had of you."

He still had pictures of her? Wait, what did she care? "If that's true, then why didn't you call the cops?"

"I did. But she told them that *I* had been harassing *her*. I even showed them my room, but she denied ever being in there and even told them she had an alibi that she'd been gone during the time that happened and that she'd just gotten back. They believed her. The only reason I didn't get arrested right then was Don, one of the ranch employees, told them that she'd done the same thing to him and a few of the other ranch hands as well."

Shelby's body shook a chill. Both from the cold and what she was hearing.

Ryker removed his jacket and draped it across her shoulders. She wanted to yank it off, but she was freezing. Heat from Ryker's body clung to the fabric, reaching out to her shivering spirit. It permeated her skin causing it to tingle.

"Look, if you don't believe me, you can call the Larimer county sheriff's department, and you can ask them. Or the guest ranch I worked at. They can verify what I'm telling you is the truth. I can even give you a list of the names that Tiffany did the same thing to."

Shelby didn't know what to believe. She wanted to believe Ryker, but she wasn't at all sure she could. She looked up at him. She could understand why Tiffany would want him. Ryker was one of the handsomest, kindest men she knew. However, how much of that desire had flowed the other way?

"Listen, I wouldn't have come back if I thought she was still after me. When they arrested her for trying to kill me—"

Shelby gasped. "Kill you?"

"Yes, I told you she's crazy. The sheriff assured me she'd be in jail for a long time, but apparently her daddy must have gotten her out."

"Who's her dad?"

Ryker mentioned the name of a well-known former governor. Shocked speechless, all Shelby could do was shake her head.

"Honestly, Shelby, I don't know what to do. I can't seem to shake this woman. And I'm not afraid to admit that she scares me. If you could have seen the slash marks in my pillow and bed and the rage it took to shred your pictures. She threatened to kill you too, Shelby." He shuddered. "That's why I had to stay away. I couldn't let anything happen to you. I've never been so scared in my life."

The only other time Shelby had heard Ryker admit he was afraid was when he was told he had cancer. She stared up at him. Fear shrouded his eyes. The woman must be bad news. That same fear jumped on her. Would that Tiffany woman kill her like she'd threatened?

Was Ryker still in danger too?

That last thought had her heart pounding in her ears.

She had to think of something to stop the mad woman, to help Ryker. But what? An idea flashed through her brain. "Ryker, what if we talked to Mr. Belmar. He's a powerful man too. I bet he'd help you put her away."

"I don't know. I hate to involve him." Ryker hooked his finger over his chin. "But then again, he just might be able to help. Let's go ask him." Ryker scooped her up and made his way back down through the trees.

Shelby didn't object as she relished not only the warmth of his body but the strength of his arms that made her feel secure and protected. The need to be even closer to him pressed in on her. She tucked her head into his chest. "What are you going to do if she's still there?"

"I don't know," Ryker puffed out. "I'll figure that out when I get down there. I can't call the cops because she hasn't done anything yet. Except for kiss me." Repulsion twisted his lips and he shivered again.

Shelby couldn't help herself, she softly chuckled.

"What's so funny?"

"You sure you don't want her to kiss you again?"

"Don't even joke with me about her." The look of horror on his face got Shelby to laughing again.

Short shallow breaths huffed out of Ryker.

"You can put me down now. I can walk."

"Not until I get you to the pavement," he said through panted breaths.

As soon as Ryker stepped onto the heated pavement, he set her down, but he didn't let her go. Instead, he turned her to face him. "Shelby, you believe me, don't you?"

Did she? She pondered on it a few seconds. No one could make up a story like that, could they? He did offer to give her a list of names and numbers of people who would back up his story. No one did that unless they were telling the truth. She nodded. "I do."

Ryker's cold hands cupped her face. His lips met hers. Though her body was freezing and she knew they needed to get inside where it was warm, she allowed him to kiss her for just a few moments. His exhilarating, love-filled kiss warmed her through and through.

"Well, isn't this cozy?"

Ryker yanked his lips from hers, and Shelby turned toward the sound of a woman's voice.

The gun was the first thing she saw.

A gun!

This wasn't some scene out of a movie, this was a real gun pointed at them.

Shelby's throat and mouth went dry.

Fear skittered through her body causing it to tremble.

Her legs threatened to give out. She hung onto Ryker for support.

"Put the gun down, Tiffany," Ryker said as he started to shift Shelby behind him.

Shelby refused to let his body shield her. She moved in front of Ryker and allowed her body to shield his instead.

"Shelby, get behind me," he ordered through a whisper, his firm voice brooking no argument. He tried to settle her behind him again, but Shelby fought against it.

"Well, isn't that something. She doesn't want to see you splattered all over the pavement. But, this little ole gun," Tiffany waved the handgun around, "will take both of you out. Remember, Darling, I told you that if I couldn't have you, no one else would either. I also told you that if I ever found that woman in the pictures, I'd kill her too. And I never forget a face." Tiffany pointed the gun at Shelby. "Especially hers."

Evil contorted Tiffany's face. Her lips slowly curved upward into a slithering smile as she aimed the weapon at Shelby's heart.

Shelby swallowed back the lump of fear, not just for herself, but for Ryker as well. She had no idea what to do to keep them both alive. Her mind scrambled for a solution.

What if she lunged after the gun? Maybe the woman wouldn't get off a good shot at her and Ryker, and they'd have a chance to get away.

God help me. She drew in a breath of courage and without giving it another thought she pushed off of

Ryker's body and bolted forward.

A shot rang out.

Shelby's feet went out from under her.

She fell to the ground.

She waited for the pain but none came.

With one push, she rolled on her side and looked behind her.

Ryker lay sprawled out flat on the ground.

"Dear God, no!" Shelby screamed.

"I didn't— I didn't mean to kill him. I only wanted to scare him." The gun in Tiffany's hand quaked.

Shelby's glance flew to Tiffany.

The gun hung at the crazy woman's side.

Madder than a wild bull, Shelby jumped up and rammed her body into Tiffany's, knocking them both to the ground, and sending the weapon into the snow several feet away. Shelby straddled Tiffany's body, and the slit in her dress ripped upward even further.

"Get off me!" Tiffany screamed and kicked, but Shelby sat on her and held the woman's arms down. All that time in the gym lifting weights was finally paying off.

"What's going on out here?"

Shelby refused to take her eyes off of Tiffany to see who had asked that. "This woman shot Ryker." Wishing she could rush to Ryker, she stayed right where she was—atop the squirming figure. She didn't want to risk Tiffany getting away and grabbing the gun again. She couldn't.

"No, I didn't," Tiffany squealed. "She did. I tried to stop her, but I was too late."

"What?" Shelby glanced at the crowd that was gathering, then yanked her gaze back to Tiffany. "Ryker was right. You are crazy."

"Help me," Tiffany whined. "Somebody help me. She's trying to kill me too."

One of the men snatched Shelby off of Tiffany and held her hands behind her back as if she were a common criminal. Shelby twisted to be able to speak to him. "You don't believe her, do you?" Shock rippled through her body and her voice.

Sitting up on the pavement, Tiffany continued to act like the victim, tears and all. "I didn't think she would kill him…"

Shelby couldn't believe this was happening to her. To Ryker. "Ryker!" Her gaze flew over to him, still lying there, not moving.

Two men were squatted down beside him.

Twisting forward and down, Shelby broke free from the man's grasp and darted toward Ryker. "Don't let her get away," she hollered over her shoulder. "*She's* the one who shot him." Shelby's glance flew to Tiffany.

Tim snatched Tiffany up by the arm and pinned her hands behind her back. The woman's screaming, kicking fit faded as Tim led her away from the crowd.

Two steps and Shelby reached Ryker. He never moved, and Shelby knew enough not to move him. She spun and scanned the crowd quickly and pointed to Mr. McIntyre. "Mr. McIntyre call 911."

"On my way." He whirled and headed to the lodge.

Shelby yelled after him, "Grab some blankets too!"

He waved in acknowledgement.

With one motion, Shelby grabbed up Ryker's coat which had fallen in the melee, and she laid it over his upper body. The two men next to Ryker removed their coats and placed them on him too.

She dropped to her knees beside him. "Ryker, can you hear me?"

No response.

She said his name again as she pressed her fingers against his neck, praying like she never had before. His pulse throbbed beneath her fingers. Setting her cheek next to his mouth, she felt the warm air as he exhaled.

The muscles in her body relaxed.

"Shelby? Shelby? What's going on?"

Half-twisting from him, Shelby watched with relief as Hailey and Jeff came sprinting through the crowd. "Ryker's been shot."

"What?" Hailey rushed to her side. "I'm an EMTI, please, give us some room."

The two gentlemen rose and stepped out of the way, pushing the crowd back as they did.

Opposite of Shelby, Hailey dropped to the ground, party dress or not. She checked for a pulse. Shelby didn't tell her that she already done that because she wanted to make sure her hope hadn't imagined one.

"I got a pulse."

Shelby nodded.

"He'll be okay, Shelby," Jeff said kneeling next to her. "He's tough."

Shelby wanted to believe Jeff, but Tiffany's gun was big enough to kill an elephant.

Her gaze slid to Ryker's face. She leaned over and

whispered in his ear, "Ryker, please don't die. I love you. I'm sorry I didn't believe you. Please, please, don't leave me again. I couldn't bear it." Her body shivered, and her shoulders ached from the cold biting into her exposed skin.

"Here, Shelby." Jeff draped his jacket around her shoulders.

"Thanks." Shelby slipped her arms into its sleeves, glad for its warmth. In the next second, she raised both of Ryker's eyelids. They were equal in size. That was the best she could do for now without a light.

Shelby continued to ask Ryker if he could hear her while she watched Hailey whip the jacket back on Ryker and began to examine his torso for the gunshot wound. Hailey shook her head. After checking his lower extremities, Hailey shook her head a second time. "There's no wound."

"What do you mean?" Shelby asked, yanking her gaze from his face to her friend's.

"Nothing." Hailey continued to examine him. "I don't feel anything. There's no blood. No hole. Nothing."

Hailey not finding a gunshot wound stumped her. Shelby went over the scenario of what happened in her mind.

The gun went off.

Ryker went down.

Could the bullet have hit him in the back as he spun?

Shelby debated whether to turn him over and search for a wound in the back. But the problem with turning him was if he had a neck injury, she could paralyze him for life. The thought of Ryker paralyzed nauseated her. *God, show me what to do?* she asked before turning her attention to her friend. "Hailey, do we dare turn him to expose his back?"

Hailey looked at her with sympathetic eyes. "Do we have a choice?"

She shook her head and drew in a deep breath. "I'll take the head. You take the shoulders. Jeff, could you please go down to his hips? On the count of three we'll logroll him gently." Shelby scooted around until she was situated at the top of his head. She reached down and put her hands around the back of his head above his neck to stabilize it for the move. She felt warm, moist stickiness in his hair.

Blood.

Please, Lord, no.

She gazed up at her friends, unable to keep the panic out of her voice. "I feel blood."

"Let's get him over." Hailey's voice held a panic of its own. "Ready."

They nodded.

"One, two, three." They rolled him onto his side, careful to keep his body and spine in alignment.

Shelby leaned over to assess the bloody area, while Hailey checked his back.

"Nothing here," Hailey said.

"I can't tell if it's a bullet wound or not." Shelby strained harder to get a good look at where the blood was coming from.

In the distance she heard the wail of sirens.

They turned Ryker to his back as carefully as they had turned him before.

Within minutes, red and white lights flashed in the driveway. The ambulance had arrived.

Shelby and Hailey gave the ambulance crew a rundown of what they'd done and found and what they hadn't.

The crew got to work, just as the sheriff arrived, and Shelby hovered as close as if there wouldn't be questions for her.

The sheriff pushed his way through the crowd and strode to where the ambulance crew hovered. "What's going on here?"

Shelby hurried to him and she noticed Tim dragging Tiffany kicking and screaming their direction. "That woman," she pointed to Tiffany only feet away from her now, "tried to kill me and Ryker."

"She's lying!" Tiffany tried to break free from Tim, but Tim had a firm grip on her.

"No, she isn't." The valet who had parked Ryker's vehicle when they'd arrived stepped up to the officer.

Another cop car showed up, and each officer took turns questioning the valet, Shelby, Tiffany, the other three valets, and several others including Tim and Mr. McIntyre separately.

In between questioning, Shelby's attention kept sliding to Ryker.

The sheriff walked over to her.

"Please, I have to follow him. He's my..." she wanted to say fiancé but that wasn't true. "I've known him all my life, and I'd like to go in the ambulance with him."

"You're free to go. You're story's been confirmed."

"Thank you." Shelby rushed over to where the ambulance was parked.

The EMT's were getting him ready for transport.

Shelby pleaded with them to let her ride up front since the one EMT would be in back with Ryker. They called dispatch to get permission and they let her because she was a search and rescue team member along with being an EMT.

Hailey ran and grabbed Shelby's coat, and she and Jeff promised to see that the benefit continued as Ryker had planned.

Inside the ambulance, Shelby watched as the county sheriff cuffed Tiffany and put her in his squad car. Even her dad wouldn't be able to get her out of this one. This was attempted murder. And all four valet's had come forth saying they had witnessed the whole thing.

On the way to the hospital, Shelby called her parents, told them what was going on, and asked if they would call Ryker's parents. They said they would and that they'd meet her at the hospital with a change of clothes. They also said that they would be praying for her and that they would call everyone else they knew to pray for Ryker too.

When they arrived at the hospital, the minute Shelby stepped inside the automatic doors of the ER, she almost gagged at the strong smell of rubbing alcohol and antiseptics.

She started to follow the EMT's, but the man with dark hair who had tended to Ryker on the trip stopped her. "Sorry, ma'am, but you can't go with us."

She nodded, fighting the numb disbelief threatening to overtake her. What she really wanted to do was yell at them and tell them she had to be with him, she just had to. However, putting her own wishes and desires aside, she knew the most important thing now was simply someone taking care of him.

"You'll have to wait out there for him." He pointed in the direction of the waiting room.

Not at all wanting to, Shelby forced her feet to move that direction. Once there, she paced back and forth, hardly feeling the movement, praying that Ryker would be okay, begging God to not let him die.

A country Christmas special flashed across the TV. Everyone was singing and having a good time. Normally she enjoyed the specials, but this one grated across her nerves. She mashed the TV's off button. With her arms across her chest, she stared out the window into the cold, dark, lonely world beyond, feeling so alone she wanted to cry.

Her heart asked the question, what if she'd found Ryker again only to lose him? What if he didn't make it? What if...? Unable to bear the thoughts, she turned away from the window to find her parents walking into the room. "Mom! Dad!" She rushed over to them, threw her arms around them, and the dam of tears she had been holding burst open.

For several minutes, she stayed in their arms, drawing comfort from their love and strength. When they separated, her mom reached in her coat pocket, pulled out a packet of tissues and handed them to Shelby.

Shelby wiped her eyes and blew her nose.

"Shelby, are you okay, kitten?" Concern creased her father's forehead. "After you called us, we heard what had happened. You saved Ryker's life, you know?"

"I just did what any EMT would do."

"No. I'm not talking about that."

Huh? What was he talking about then?

"When you shoved off of Ryker to charge that woman, you knocked him off balance and he hit the ground. If you hadn't, that bullet would have hit him square."

She wiped at her eyes again, trying to piece together what her father was saying. "How—how do you know that?"

"Because they found the bullet right behind him embedded in a tree."

The nausea returned full force as the reality of just how close Ryker really had come to taking that bullet pummeled into her consciousness.

"I'm so proud of you, kitten." Her father pulled her into his arms.

Words she'd longed to hear for so long brought a fresh onslaught of tears, and it wrenched heart-rending sobs from her.

"Shelby, what's wrong? Did I say something wrong?"

She shook her head no against her daddy's chest. The same chest she'd cuddled against so many times as a young girl. "No, Dad, you didn't. You said exactly what I needed to hear." She pulled back far enough to look into her father's face. "I thought you were disappointed in me because I wasn't a boy."

"What?" His eyes widened in horror. "I never... I didn't..." He pulled her close again. "Oh, kitten. I'm so sorry you felt that way. Yes, I wanted a boy. But, I wouldn't trade a million boys for you. I love you. You're the best daughter a man could ever ask for."

Euphoria and acceptance touched that place in her soul that had been wounded for so long, caressing it with healing. Sniffles sounded from beside her. Shelby pulled away to see her mother brushing away the tears from under her eyes.

Shelby left the circle of her dad's embrace and gave her mother a hug. She was so blessed to have parents who were there for her, who loved her, and whom she loved. When they broke apart, Shelby asked her mom, "Do you think Ryker's going to be okay?"

"I don't know, honey, but God does. So why don't we pray?"

The three of them joined hands and prayed for God to perform a miracle. Shelby hoped He was listening because she never wanted to be without Ryker again. She just hoped it wasn't too late for that already.

Chapter Eleven

The ambulance crew that had brought Ryker in walked by the waiting room, pushing their gurney, and heading toward the emergency room exit. Knowing they might know something, Shelby rushed out after them and tried to catch up to them to thank them, but she stopped suddenly when she overheard the younger one of them say to the other, "As hard as he hit his head, I wonder if that poor guy fractured his skull or if he has a small brain bleed."

Fractured skull?

Brain bleed?

Knowing those two things were definite possibilities with a head injury, dread and fear plopped into her heart. Choking back a sob, she whirled and fled to the restroom. She stood in front of the mirror, staring at her reflection. First thing she noticed was the diagonal tear in the shoulder of her black gown. Her eyes drifted lower to the rip that exposed her leg and most of her thigh. Chunks of hair had come undone from on top of her head. She looked like she'd been attacked. And in a way she had been only she had been the one doing the attacking.

But none of that mattered now. With no one else in the room, she stared at her reflection and admonished herself. "Listen, Shelby, this is no time for you to break down. You've got to be brave for Ryker's sake. You can do this."

"You sure can." Her mother came into the bathroom just as the last four words left Shelby's mouth.

"Oh, Mom." Shelby threw her arms around her mother. "What if Ryker doesn't make it?"

"He will, sweetie. God will take care of him."

But Shelby wasn't sure she even believed that anymore. "Sometimes, I don't think God cares one way or another."

"Now, Shelby, how can you say that?" Compassion, not shock or condemnation, brushed through her mother's voice.

"Because, Mom. When Ryker left, I prayed and prayed that he would come back. After a year of praying, I finally stopped believing that God even cared about me."

"What?" Compassion pillowed the word. "Of course, He cares about you."

She swiped at the tears, sniffing them back as anger toppled over them. "Yeah, well, He has a funny way of showing it."

"Why? Because you didn't get the answer you wanted when you prayed?"

Shelby shrugged. "You know, Mom, I thought that was the point— if I prayed, God would fix it. He's the only One that could. And He didn't. I don't know what to think anymore."

"Oh Shelby, honey, that's not what prayer is about." Her mother took her hand. "First of all, prayer is about communicating with God. It's about trusting Him with the situation or the problem even when you don't get the result you want. Trusting that He has your best interest."

"How could it be in my best interest that Ryker left me?"

"I don't know. How could it? What have you learned through that?"

"Are you're saying that God did this to teach me something?" Astonishment and anger struck through her like bolts of lightning.

"No, I'm saying God uses the things that happen to teach us that His love is always there for us—in the good times and even in the bad times. He never leaves us nor forsakes us no matter what. Did you read the story about Joseph like I asked you to?"

She didn't want to admit it because although she had, she hadn't really gotten much out of it. "Yes."

"Well, look at all that Joseph went through, and the Bible says that *the Lord was with Joseph*. Our mind says how can that be? Joseph was just a seventeen-year-old kid. He had everything he needed and wanted. He had a family. A father who loved him. Who favored him above his other children, and who doted on him. Then one day, all that Joseph knew was taken from him in an instant. He was pitched down a well and sold into slavery.

"During all of that, the Lord was with him. That means He was with him when his brothers tossed him into that well. He was with Joseph when they sold him into slavery, when he was next to the throne, and even when he was tossed into prison. God was there with him in the valleys and on the mountaintops. The Lord never left him." Her mother cupped her chin. "Shelby, honey, we don't see the whole picture, but God does. Look how things ended up for Joseph. A whole nation was spared from a severe famine because of him." She dropped her hand.

"But why didn't God do it differently? Why did God make Joseph go through all that just to save a nation?"

"God didn't do it to Joseph. His brothers did."

"But God could have stopped it."

"Do you want to marry Ryker?"

"Huh? What does that have to do with Joseph?"

"Answer me, Shelby. Do you?"

"Yes. Of course I do. Why?"

"Well, what if God came in and took over your will and didn't let you marry Ryker. Would you like that? Would you like God to override your will and force you to do things you don't want to do?"

"No."

"Exactly. God didn't override Joseph's brothers' will's either. What He did do, was give Joseph favor and turn things around for him. Just like He's done for you, honey. Ryker's here now and so is God. God has always been here, during your lows and your highs, waiting for an opportunity to make good of your life."

Shelby thought about that.

The bathroom door opened and an elderly lady gave them a sad smile and headed into one of the stalls.

"Thanks, Mom. I love you." She hugged her mother, and they headed back out to the waiting room.

Halfway there, her dad met them, carrying a small duffle bag. "Here's the clothes we brought for you. You might want to hurry up and change. They've taken Ryker up to the ICU, and they said you could see him there, but only for a few minutes."

Shelby snatched the bag and headed back into the bathroom into one of the stalls. As fast as she could, she changed into her white cashmere sweater, gray, wool slacks and socks, and her black, high-heeled, winter boots. She wadded up her dress and stuffed it and her heels into her duffle bag. From the side pocket of it, she removed her brush and quickly ran it through her hair. She gathered her hair and held it together with a scrunchie, then put the brush back into the bag. The transformation took mere minutes.

"I'm ready," she said, stepping out into the hallway.

The three of them made their way to ICU with Shelby leading the pack.

"Shelby, slow down. We're not running a marathon." Her mother's voice floated from behind her.

Shelby didn't want to slow down, but out of respect for her parents, she did. She also prayed the whole way there. Only this time, she prayed with more confidence, knowing God was with her and Ryker no matter what.

Up at the ICU unit, Shelby's parents stayed in the ICU waiting area while she made her way to Ryker's room. Each step she took closer to the room, her heart beat faster and faster. What would she find when she got there?

Her stride slowed as she stepped into his room. Disinfectant odors met her there.

Hooked up to machines and monitors, Ryker lay in the bed, unmoving. Her heart wept. She couldn't help it. Helplessness cascaded over her in such torrents that she could hardly breathe through them.

Her soul tugged her in two different directions.

Flee.

Stay.

Flee.

Stay.

She wanted to do both because part of her wondered how she could ever have the strength to face this. But the call of her heart was stronger. It wanted to be near him.

To talk to him.

To hear his voice.

To see him open those blue eyes of his.

After seconds of battling, fleeing lost, letting go so suddenly that she was propelled forward.

She stepped to the side of his bed, and over the bedrail, she reached for his hand that was lying on top of the folded down sheet. When she touched him, he didn't move or even flinch.

When she leaned down and pressed her lips to his cheek, a mixture of antiseptics and a faint citrusy pine scent slipped into her nostrils. "Ryker, it's me, Shelby. Can you hear me?"

Nothing.

"Ryker, please open your eyes?"

Nothing.

Her tears, unbidden fell onto his hospital gown.

* * *

The rest of the day, and most of the next, Shelby took whatever moments the nurse's station would give her with him. Each moment she spent with him, it became harder and harder to see him lying there motionless, unresponsive. Even worse, was not knowing what was wrong him, or if he was even going to live or die.

Beep. Beep. Beep. The heart monitor filled the silence as she sat next to his bed, holding his hand.

If only the nurses would tell her something, anything. But they refused to tell her anything medical because she wasn't family. Stupid medical privacy act law. At one point, she even thought about lying and telling them that she was his fiancée, but lying was wrong no matter what the motive.

For the hundredth time her eyes raked over him. Her heart ached seeing him like this. Helplessness, hopelessness, and despair visited her in that room. She wished she could trade places with him. It was pure torture knowing there wasn't a single thing she could do to help the man she loved. She felt completely powerless where Ryker was concerned.

Then suddenly, as if a bright light had flashed through her brain, she got it. She finally understood exactly how Ryker had felt and why he had left. Up until now, she never really understood it. Even when he was up on the mountain in that snow cave, she didn't. But, here, right now, in this moment, seeing him lying there unconscious and not being able to do a thing about it made her feel absolutely hopeless and useless. How did Ryker ever endure watching Randy like this for months on end, and how had he felt at the end when Randy finally let go for that last breath?

Horror knifed through her at the thought of sitting here watching Ryker like that.

She thought back to that time when Randy had gotten ill. She'd been away at college. She and Ryker weren't even dating at the time. So she'd never really seen Randy or the torment Ryker had surely gone through.

Hooking her hands on Ryker's bedrail, Shelby bowed her head between her arms and closed her eyes. Tears fell onto her lap as her heart ached for what Ryker must have gone through, and how hard it had to have been on him to watch the brother he adored suffer and die.

How hard it must have been for him to say goodbye to Randy. How hard it must have been for him to say goodbye to her like he did. "I'm sorry, Ryker. I'm so sorry for not understanding."

"Shelby?" A hand settled on her shoulder.

Slowly and wobbly as if she really might be caught in the clutches of a dream, she raised her tear-stained face toward the voice. "Mrs. Anderson?" Shelby leapt up and threw her arms around Ryker's mother, a woman Shelby loved almost as much as her own. "I'm so glad you're here."

"How is he?" Her gray-blue eyes, the same color as Ryker's, shifted to her son.

Shelby stepped out of the way and allowed the woman to stand next to Ryker's bedside while she went and stood at the end of the bed.

"Ryker, honey, it's me, Mother." Mrs. Anderson ran her hand over the dark stubble on his face.

No response.

Shelby's heart dropped to her stomach. She had hoped once his mother arrived that he would respond to her.

"Your dad's here too, son."

"Do I need to leave so Mr. Anderson can come in?"

Mrs. Anderson's glance went to Shelby. "No, he's with your parents now, telling them about Ryker's medical diagnosis."

"Did they tell you what is wrong with him?" Hope slipped into her heart.

"Yes." Mrs. Anderson faced Shelby.

She had to ask, she had to know. She'd waited so long to hear his prognosis. "Please, Mrs. Anderson, I have to know. Is he going to be all right?" Shelby held her breath, waiting and yet fearing the answer at the same time.

"Oh, Shelby, didn't they tell you anything?" She moved toward Shelby and put her arm around her slumped shoulders.

"No." Shelby shook her head. "They couldn't."

"I'm so sorry, Shelby. They believe he's going to be just fine once the swelling goes down. Other than the laceration on the back of his head, he has a severe concussion, but they do expect him to recover."

"He doesn't have a fractured skull, or a small brain bleed?"

Mrs. Anderson frowned. "What gave you that idea?"

Her own stupidity, by listening to and taking to heart, a conversation that wasn't meant for her.

Shelby closed her eyes, her knees turned to liquid.

She backed up to the chair behind her and sat down. "Oh, thank you. And thank you, Lord."

A moment and she gazed up at Mrs. Anderson. "I can't tell you how glad I am to hear that. I've been so worried about him. Thank you." She rose. "I'll go out now so Mr. Anderson can come in."

"Shelby, before you go, I just want to say I'm so glad that you and Ryker are working things out. He loves you, you know? The last eighteen months have been very hard on him. As, I'm sure, they have been on you. I hope you understand why he left the way he did."

She should be going, but the two of them needed to get this said. "To be honest with you, when he first told me, I didn't. But seeing him like this and knowing that he went through so much worse, I have to say. Now I completely understand."

Ryker's mother grabbed Shelby and pulled her into her arms. "I'm so glad."

"Me too." They pulled back and each of them smiled through their moist eyes. "Okay, well, I'm going to go get something to eat. I can finally do that knowing that you're here and that he's going to be okay."

"When's the last time you ate?" Concern edged into her eyes.

Shelby thought about it for a moment. "Yesterday?"

Mrs. Anderson gasped with concern. "Oh, honey, you mean you haven't eaten anything since yesterday?"

"No, I couldn't. But now, all of a sudden, I'm starving." Feeling lighter than she had in days, Shelby kissed Ryker's cheek, and then went out into the waiting area. She talked to Mr. Anderson for a few minutes, and then she and her parents went downstairs to get a bite to eat.

They stepped into the elevator and pushed the cafeteria floor's number.

"You heard he's going to be okay, right, kitten?" her dad asked from beside her.

She looked up at him and smiled. "Yes, Mrs. Anderson told me." Her attention went to her mother. "You were right, Mom. God's been with both us through this whole thing."

Her mother smiled that knowing smile of hers. The one that always comforted Shelby.

* * *

That evening Shelby went home and slept for the first time in two days. She woke up the next morning with an idea swirling through her brain.

She tossed the covers aside, slid her feet into her slippers, grabbed her robe and put it on, then she and Max headed toward the smell of frying bacon and coffee.

Her mom stood at the stove stirring something. Her dad was either not up yet or in the shower because he wasn't anywhere around. "Morning, Mom, how would you like to plan a Christmas wedding?"

The sizzling bacon was drowned out with her mom's voice. "Mornin— A what?" The spatula in her mother's hand stopped mid-air. "Did Ryker propose again? Wait, how could he? He's been in a coma. Did he propose at the benefit party before he…? Or when? I don't understand." Her mom's brows dipped in confusion.

Shelby giggled at the fast-firing questions. "No, Mom, he didn't propose. I'm going to propose to him."

Her mom's eyes bulged, and her mouth dropped open. It wasn't often her mom was speechless.

"I know the man usually proposes, but Ryker did it once before, and I'm not letting him get away again, so I'm not taking any chances. I'm going to propose to him as soon as he wakes up."

Her mother's eyes widened even further. "Seriously?"

"That's my word, Mom. And yes, I'm serious. I'm also going to go ahead and start making wedding plans for Christmas Eve Day right away. It'll be a small wedding with just you and Dad and Mr. and Mrs. Anderson and a few of our friends."

"Mercy me, you are serious. But where can you even get a building on such short notice?"

"Right here." She waved her hand to span her large living area, and mother's eyes followed her movement.

"With all the Christmas decorations and the fireplace and that beautiful Christmas tree, it would make a great place to have a wedding." Her mother's attention yanked back to Shelby. "But what if… What if Ryker isn't out of the hospital by then?"

Shelby settled a finger against her lip and frowned. "Hmmm, I don't know. That would be a problem. Well, I'll just wait a couple of days and see how things go. If he's better by then, and says yes to my proposal, then between the two of us," Shelby winked twice. "Hint, hint." She smiled. "We could get everything done in a hurry, couldn't we?"

This smile was almost certain. "We sure could. After all, I've thrown bigger parties than that together in less time."

"Great." Shelby clasped her hands together. "I knew I could count on you. Thanks, Mom." That settled, Shelby was ready to eat. "What's for breakfast?" She peered into the pan. "Um, not that."

Mom glanced at the pan. "Oh, dear." She yanked the skillet up from the stove and turned the burner off. "Burnt eggs don't sound very appealing, do they?"

"Um, no." They laughed.

"How are my two favorite women this morning?" Her father came into the room all freshly shaven and showered.

"Great," her mother said before Shelby could say anything. "Shelby's getting married."

Her dad whipped his neck around so fast Shelby thought it would snap. "She's what?"

Again, she giggled.

They quickly explained their plans, and he readily agreed and even offered to help.

After a quick breakfast of bagels with cream cheese, crispy bacon strips, no eggs, and coffee, they headed to the hospital in Shelby's SUV.

When they arrived at the ICU, the nurse on duty rushed to them. Shelby's heart sank. "What's wrong?"

"He's awake, and he's been asking for you." The nurse smiled. "His parents are with him now, but as soon as one of them leaves, you can go in. I'll tell them you're here." She whirled and scurried into Ryker's room.

"He's awake!" The three of them hugged.

"You can go in now," the nurse informed them. "Mr. Anderson said he'd leave as soon as you go in."

Shelby hurried to his room.

After greeting his parents and hugging them, both of them made their way to the door. "We'll go and give you two some time alone.

Her attention skidded across to Ryker. His eyes were opened, not wide, but wide enough, and a weak smile drifted across his face.

"Shelby." He held his hand toward her.

Hearing him say her name, Shelby's heart skipped. She rushed to his side, as the Anderson's slipped out of the room, leaving her alone with Ryker.

* * *

The back of Ryker's head hurt with a throbbing he wasn't sure he could fight off, but Shelby was a sight for sore eyes.

Her soft hand wrapped around his, and he gave it a light squeeze.

"Oh, Ryker, I'm so glad you're awake. I was so worried about you, so afraid of losing you again."

"No way. That'll never happen." His words came out raspy. He reached for the hospital glass with the straw, but Shelby beat him to it. He raised his head to take a sip and winced.

"Do I need to call the nurse?" She reached for the call button.

"No." He raised his hand. "They'll only give me

more pain meds, and those things put me to sleep. I don't want to sleep right now. I want to talk to you."

Her eyes caressed him, so incredibly glad to just be able to look at him. "I want to talk to you too. Before I do though, how are you feeling?"

"Like someone hit me over the head."

"Someone did. Me."

He frowned.

"Well, kind of, sort of. When I went to charge that woman, I guess I shoved off of you pretty hard and it sent you flying backward."

"From what I was told," he rasped. "You saved my life."

"I can't take credit for that. God did it."

"Shelby, if you hadn't of shoved me down, Tiffany's bullet would have hit me."

"That's what they said." She brushed it off as if it made her uncomfortable.

He hadn't meant to make her feel that way, but how could he not say anything? Her bravery had saved his life.

"I'm sorry for leaving you—" he said, wishing he was stronger. Every word was an uphill fight.

"Oh, Ryker," she blurted, stopping him from what he was about to say. "I—I—" Her eyes filled with tears.

"Hey, don't cry." He pulled her hand closer to his chest. "Everything will be okay. You'll see."

"No, Ryker, I'm sorry, I didn't understand why you left. I tried, but I just couldn't. Until now." Her eyes met his, and in them was understanding mixed with ache. "Seeing you here like this... I didn't know how hard it would be. And knowing there was nothing I could do to help you or to make you better about drove me crazy. I have never felt so helpless or so scared in my life."

"Ah, darling, I'm sorry. Can you ever forgive me for putting you through all this?"

"Please, don't be sorry. And it's not you who needs to ask for forgiveness, it's me." She kissed his hand and clutched it to her. "Can you ever forgive me for not understanding? For thinking the worst?"

"Only if you will forgive me too."

She nodded, then turned away. In two steps, she grabbed the ugly gold chair and pulled it up alongside his bed. She placed one knee on it and picked up his hand again. "Ryker Anderson, I don't ever want to be without you again. I love you with all my heart, and I want to be with you forever. Until death do us part, however long or short that may be. Ryker, my darling, will you marry me?"

With no real grasp of where she had been going with that speech, Ryker couldn't keep his mouth from falling open on the last question. Had he heard her correctly or was the bump on his head causing him to hallucinate and to hear things? "Did, did you just ask me to marry you?" His voice barely came out above a whisper.

Her half-smile was couched with a bit of fear. "Yes, I did. What do you say? Will you marry me?" Uncertainty clouded her big brown eyes.

"Shelby, darling, you know I'll marry you. I love you too. Now kiss me." He sent her a playful smirk of a smile. "But be gentle."

In less than one heartbeat, in one push, Shelby

shoved the chair out of the way and claimed his lips. His heart soared like wings of an eagle. Nothing had ever felt so right or so good.

When she raised her mouth off of his, he pulled her head back down. "I'm not finished kissing you yet. Don't know if I ever will be," he rasped against her lips.

"Oh, I like the way you think." Their mouths melded together.

When the kiss ended, Shelby gazed down at him. "So, I was thinking about a Christmas wedding. What do you think?"

Concern dropped into him. "Christmas? I don't want to waste another year. I want to us to be man and wife as soon as possible."

"Good, then we agree."

"Huh?" Even with a massive headache, he was pretty sure she made no sense. "Didn't you hear what I said? I said—"

Her fingertips covered his lips. "I heard every word, and I agree. I talked to Mom this morning to see if she could help me plan a wedding by Christmas. This Christmas."

"Man, you don't waste any time, do you?" His lips curved upward, and joy did a jig across his heart.

"Nope."

"So you were that positive that I'd say yes, huh?" Mirth sprinkled through his eyes.

"Yep." She smiled smugly at him. Then her smile slipped, replaced by a frown and a shake of her head. "No, not really. Just hopeful."

"Shelby." He brought her hand to his lips and kissed

it. "I love you. Don't you ever doubt that again, you hear? I can't wait to marry you. If the doc says yes, and even if he doesn't, we're getting married Christmas Day." Christmas Day couldn't come soon enough for him.

Epilogue

Christmas Day had finally arrived.

Stars filled the night sky.

Snow covered the ground. It was only eight degrees outside, but Shelby was nice and warm. Not just because she was inside, but because she was about to live her dream of becoming Ryker's wife.

She stood in front of the full-length mirror at the Anderson's lodge. When people got wind of her and Ryker's wedding, the list of people who wanted to come, grew. So, they ended up having it here instead of at her house. At first, Shelby wasn't sure how she felt about that with all that had happened here with that woman. But Tiffany was long gone, and for good this time.

Shelby turned one way and then the other, admiring her princess wedding dress. The halter neckline and ruffled wool-standing collar covered half of the back of her head and scooped to a V in the front.

The long sleeves belled right below the elbow, and the same fluffy wool lined the top of the bell and beaded lace lined the bottom of them.

Each satin layer of her skirt was different. The top layer was bunched and had the same beaded lace that was around the bottom of her sleeves. The second layer flowed from under the first, reminding her of the tails on a scarf dress.

Tulle material covered the full belled skirt with the straight hem.

She'd purchased this dress when Ryker had asked her to marry him the first time. A winter wedding had always been her dream, and now it was coming true.

But what if…? Panic stuck into her and held there like a hat pin. "Mom, Ryker's here, right?"

"Yes, honey. He's waiting downstairs for you."

Shelby let out the breath she held.

"And he's not waiting very patiently either." Hailey extended Shelby's bouquet of powder-blue roses, white roses, and pine bough. "Now take this thing already, and let's get going."

"Pushy." Shelby wrinkled her nose at her friend.

"Yep, I sure am." Hailey smiled at her. "By the way you look fabulous."

"Thanks. You look pretty nice yourself." And she did too in that soft blue flowing gown.

"You ready, kitten?" her dad asked from the other side of the door. "Everyone's waiting."

Her mother opened the door, and her father stood on the other side looking quite debonair with his slightly graying temples and his neatly pressed black tuxedo.

Her dad looked Shelby up and down, and his face beamed. "You look beautiful, kitten."

"Thank you, Daddy."

"Daddy? I haven't heard you call me that in a long time. Sounds good to this old man's ears. Especially today."

"Why today? And you're not old." Shelby shook her head.

"Well, I'm losing my girl to another man. You won't be daddy's little girl anymore."

Shelby went to his side and kissed her dad on the cheek. "I'll always be daddy's little girl. Nothing will ever change that."

He nodded, and his eyes glistened.

"Now don't you go crying or I'll start too, and it will ruin my makeup," Shelby admonished him with a sniff.

"I'm not crying. I have something in my eye." He pressed his finger and thumb over his eyes and sniffed.

Hiking her shoulders, Shelby let the excitement of the day overtake her. "Just think, Dad. Today you'll get the son you always wanted." Days ago, those words would have driven a spike into her heart, but today, knowing her daddy was proud of her, and that he wouldn't trade her for a whole houseful of boys, it didn't bother her at all.

"I sure will. But I already have something even better than a son. I have you."

Shelby's heart swelled, and she kissed her dad on the cheek again.

"Hello. Are you two going to stand there all day or are you coming?" her mom asked, standing by the door, dabbing at her eyes with a tissue.

Together they walked to the door and watched from inside the room as her mom headed down the long staircase. Scott, one of Ryker's friends, held out his hand and escorted her to the front and past the row of seats filled to capacity with guests.

Next Hailey went.

Jeff waited at the bottom of the stairs to escort her.

His smile almost covered his whole beaming face, and his eyes never left Hailey.

"You ready, Max?" Shelby glanced down at her dog. "You look so cute in that tux." She wagged her finger at him playfully. "Now don't you go chewing on that ring pillow, you hear me? And when I tell you to, you give it to Ryker, okay?"

Max sat there staring up at her with his one blue eye and one brown. Hanging from Max's neck was a white satin pillow with their wedding bands tied in place by a powder-blue ribbon.

Finally, it was time for them to go.

Her father wove Shelby's hand through his arm and led her to the top of the stairs. Max walked beside them. At the top of the landing, she looked down and her heart skipped when she saw Ryker.

He's really here. As much as she hated for it to, the fear of him not showing up had stayed with her right up until the second she laid eyes on him.

Happiness and joy bubbled through her.

Ryker, my darling, I'm coming.

* * *

Ryker stood in the front of the room. The lights from the massive Christmas tree only a mere eight-feet behind him twinkled. Hundreds of light blue candles and sparkling Christmas lights provided the only lighting in the place. But, there were enough of them that one could see pretty well.

He looked over at his parents. His mother blotted the

corner of her eyes, her smile, one of happiness and not sadness. His mother who had only two sons had always wanted a daughter, and now she was going to have one.

Violin music floated through the air.

All the chattering stopped.

Ryker's gaze went to the end of the row.

Scott escorted Shelby's mother to the front and seated her, then he took a seat behind her.

Next, Hailey and Jeff strolled down the aisle, arm-in-arm. When they reached Ryker, Hailey went one way and Jeff went the other.

When *Unchained Melody* began to play, Ryker's focus drifted to the top of the staircase.

There stood Shelby looking more beautiful than he'd ever seen her before. Peace and happiness grabbed his spirit and joy split right through him. Her hand slid down the log rail as she slowly descended with her dad on one side and Max just in front of them.

Ryker grinned. He still couldn't believe her search and rescue dog was their ring bearer. But, Shelby loved that dog, and he did too. Gratitude filled his heart for both of them. If it wasn't for Max and Shelby, he wouldn't even be here today. And he wouldn't be marrying the woman who possessed not only his every thought, but his heart as well.

Dressed like one of those Cinderella princesses, Shelby glided up the rows of chairs filled with their friends, family, and people from all over the county.

Ryker mentally shook his head. He couldn't believe how many people had come to celebrate Shelby and his union on Christmas Day Eve.

Their eyes connected, and he was powerless to break the connection, nor did he want to. He wanted only to be held by those eyes for the rest of his life.

"Who gives this woman in holy matrimony?" Nigel, their pastor asked.

"Her mother and I do." The connection was only broken when Mr. Davis kissed Shelby on the cheek.

His soon-to-be father-in-law placed Shelby's hand into Ryker's. "Take good care of my girl."

"You can count on it…. Dad."

A smile split across Mr. Davis's face, and his chest puffed out. "Thank you…. Son." He turned and went and sat down next to Mrs. Davis.

Ryker looked at Shelby, her smile lit up the room. "You ready for this?"

"More than ready." The love in her eyes sent strokes of love brushing across the canvas of his heart.

They took the three steps and stood in front of Nigel.

There, they promised to love one another for better or for worse, in sickness and in health, until death did them part.

"You may now kiss your bride."

Ryker pulled Shelby into his arms. Not caring that there was a room full of guests, he kissed her soundly and thoroughly.

Clapping and whoops and hollers erupted into the room.

Against her lips, eyes open, he whispered, "We'll continue this later." He winked, and Shelby's face turned a pretty shade of pink. They turned and faced their guests.

"Ladies and gentleman, I present to you now, Mr. and Mrs. Ryker Anderson."

* * *

Shelby couldn't believe her ears. She was now Mrs. Ryker Anderson. Something she hadn't thought possible eighteen months ago. But now here she was reunited at Christmas with the man who never, ever really let go of her heart.

Other Books by Debra Ullrick

Groom Wanted

It's a perfect plan-best friends Leah Bowen and Jake Lure will each advertise for mail-order spouses in the papers, and then Jake will help select Leah's future husband, while Leah picks Jake's bride-to-be! Surely the ads will find them what they seek: a wife who'll appreciate Jake's shy charm and a groom who'll take Leah away from the Idaho Territory she detests.

When the responses to the postings pour in, it seems all Leah's and Jake's dreams will soon come true. But the closer they each get to the altar, the less appealing marrying a stranger becomes. Is it too late to turn back-or to turn around and find the happiness they truly seek together, at last?

The Unexpected Bride

After the disaster of his first marriage, Haydon Bowen has no intention of marrying again. Unfortunately, his brother has some intentions of his own, and plans to see to it that Haydon finds happiness once more. So he answers a "groom wanted" advertisement—in Haydon's name—and sends Haydon to meet his new bride at the stagecoach stop!

For beautiful, cultured Rainelle Devonwood, any dangers she may face in the Idaho Territories are preferable to staying with her abusive brother. So even when Rainee learns she's a mistakenly ordered bride, she won't let Haydon drive her away. She's up to the challenge of life on the difficult, demanding frontier...and the great challenge of opening Haydon's heart again.

The Unlikely Wife

The arrival of Michael Bowen's bride, married sight unseen by proxy, sends the rancher reeling. With her trousers, cowboy hat and rifle, she looks like a female outlaw—not the genteel lady he corresponded with for months. He's been hoodwinked into marriage with the wrong woman!

Selina Farleigh Bowen loved Michael's letters, even if she couldn't read them herself. A friend read them to her, and wrote her replies—but apparently that "friend" left things out, like Michael's dream of a wife who was nothing like her. Selina won't change who she is, not even for the man she loves. Yet time might show Michael the true value of his unlikely wife.

A Log Cabin Christmas
A New York Times & CBA Bestseller

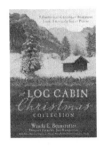 Experience Christmas through the eyes of adventuresome settlers who relied on log cabins built from trees on their own land to see them through the cruel forces of winter. Discover how rough-hewed shelters become a home in which faith, hope, and love can flourish. Marvel in the blessings of Christmas celebrations without the trappings of modern commercialism where the true meaning of the day shines through. And treasure this exclusive collection of nine Christmas romances penned by some of Christian fiction's best-selling authors.

The Unintended Groom
Colorado Courtship
Reunited at Christmas
Christmas Belles of Georgia
Dixie Hearts
The Bride Wore Coveralls
A Dozen Apologies
Forewarned
Catch Me If You Can (2014)

Visit the author's website:
www.DebraUllrick.com

About the Author

Debra Ullrick is a hot rod, figure-eight races, classic cars, mud-boggin', monster trucks fanatic, who loves Jesus. Her hobbies include, going to classic car auto shows, collecting muscle car and monster truck models, reading, writing, drawing western art, feeding wild birds, playing with her Manx cat Tickles, visiting with family and friends, surfing the Internet, watching movies, especially every available version of Jane Austen's stories, Monster Jam World Finals DVD's, Ma and Pa Kettle, Little People, Big World, CASTLE, COPS, and the PBS documentaries, Frontier House, 1900's house, and Manor House.

Debra and her real-life hero of forty years, along with their now married daughter lived and worked on cattle ranches in the Colorado Rocky Mountains until a few years ago. Now they live down in the flatlands where they're still experiencing cultural whiplash from big city living.

Her debut novel, *The Bride Wore Coveralls,* the first book in this series is available through **www.amazon.com** and numerous other places on the Internet.

Debra loves to hear from her readers.

To contact her visit her website at **www.debraullrick.com** or write her at **christianromancewriter@gmail.com.** You can find Debra on **Twitter** and **Facebook**.

Made in the USA
Charleston, SC
06 April 2015